A LOSING BATTLE

Slocum danced slowly with her in the dirt, circling around the red light. They went around smoothly as if on a polished dance floor.

"Where's my partner Heck?" he asked her under his breath. "You seen him?"

She looked up at him and grinned as if slightly embarrassed. "Oh, he and Rosa are having their own fandango."

"So I ain't lost him." Slocum laughed softly and took a better hitch on his hand around her waist. They danced away in easy circles.

"No problem," Matilda said, and looked up at him. "The señora? Paco said the Comanches kidnapped her."

"Mary's a fine lady. She lost her husband and son too."

Matilda nodded as he swung her around to the music. "It is not a good time. Both of my husbands were killed."

"Comanche?"

"Banditos the first, and maybe Indians killed the second one."

He looked off into the starlit night. The killing never stopped. The war was over and another begun—maybe more than one. The thought made his guts roil as the soft music filled the night and he spun the firm-bodied Matilda around in a circle.

Maybe, maybe they would soon be moving cattle.

JAKE LOGAN

SLOCUM

AND THE

COMANCHE CAPTIVE

JOVE BOOKS, NEW YORK

THE BERKLEY PUBLISHING GROUP
Published by the Penguin Group
Penguin Group (USA) Inc.
375 Hudson Street, New York, New York 10014, USA

Penguin Group (Canada), 90 Eglinton Avenue East, Suite 700, Toronto, Ontario M4P 2Y3, Canada
(a division of Pearson Penguin Canada Inc.)
Penguin Books Ltd., 80 Strand, London WC2R 0RL, England
Penguin Group Ireland, 25 St. Stephen's Green, Dublin 2, Ireland (a division of Penguin Books Ltd.)
Penguin Group (Australia), 250 Camberwell Road, Camberwell, Victoria 3124, Australia
(a division of Pearson Australia Group Pty. Ltd.)
Penguin Books India Pvt. Ltd., 11 Community Centre, Panchsheel Park, New Delhi—110 017, India
Penguin Group (NZ), 67 Apollo Drive, Rosedale, North Shore 0745, Auckland, New Zealand
(a division of Pearson New Zealand Ltd.)
Penguin Books (South Africa) (Pty.) Ltd., 24 Sturdee Avenue, Rosebank, Johannesburg 2196,
South Africa

Penguin Books Ltd., Registered Offices: 80 Strand, London WC2R 0RL, England

This is a work of fiction. Names, characters, places, and incidents either are the product of the author's imagination or are used fictitiously, and any resemblance to actual persons, living or dead, business establishments, events, or locales is entirely coincidental.

SLOCUM AND THE COMANCHE CAPTIVE

A Jove Book / published by arrangement with the author

PRINTING HISTORY
Jove edition / September 2007

ISBN: 978-0-515-14351-5

JOVE®
Jove Books are published by The Berkley Publishing Group,
a division of Penguin Group (USA) Inc.,
375 Hudson Street, New York, New York 10014.
JOVE is a registered trademark of Penguin Group (USA) Inc.
The "J" design is a trademark belonging to Penguin Group (USA) Inc.

PRINTED IN THE UNITED STATES OF AMERICA

10 9 8 7 6 5 4 3 2 1

1

The burro he rode wearied by the hour. Against the glare of the sun and the dazzling heat waves, he kept Judas in a dogtrot by continually beating on its butt with a stick. Streams of sweat ran from under the hatband of his weathered felt hat, down his whisker-grizzled face, and dripped off his chin. The moisture made his silk kerchief and shirt collar damp enough to cool him around his throat and chest, despite the harsh oven heat sweeping his face in blasts of wind.

The first sign of life he saw was a patch of yellow canvas stretched over some wagon bows. How many cow outfits could be out in this desolate dead mesquite and black brush? No way to know, but he suspected there weren't many. He drew closer and saw some shaggy brown mustangs, heads down and standing hip-shot, swatting flies with their long tails. Satisfied this was the cow camp he sought, he shut Judas down to a walk.

Someone came around the wagon armed with a shotgun. Bare-headed, the gun bearer looked Mexican. Slocum waved at him.

"No Comanche!" he shouted, figuring the man trusted no one—which was the best way to survive out there.

"What business you got here?" the graybeard demanded in Spanish.

"Looking for Colonel Banks." Slocum said, and set Judas down a few yards from the menacing twin barrels aimed at him.

"He's asleep."

Slocum stepped off his burro and nodded. "Don't bother him. I'll wait until he wakes up." He pulled the crotch of his pants out of his crack and gave his genitals more room. Standing straddle-legged, he looked up as a tall man came around the wagon.

"It's all right, Lopez. He's a gringo."

Lopez nodded like he knew and dropped the muzzle down.

"What can I do for you?" the gray-headed man asked with an appraising eye on Slocum.

"I could use some work. Jimmy Ray Collins said you might need some ropers down here."

The man nodded as if taking it all into consideration. In his forties, broad-shouldered, he wore buckskin pants, galluses, and a white shirt. The knee-high boots looked dusty over a good polish job. Straight-backed, he spoke with all the authority of a former colonel in the Confederacy.

"I didn't catch your name."

"Slocum."

"Well, Slocum, I pay a dollar a head for any tied-down steer that ain't got a broken neck or leg."

Slocum looked over the low thorny brush and nodded. "That include *found*?"

Banks nodded, and folded his arms. "You don't get three steers a week, you owe me for the grub. It's fifty cents a day."

"You got some good cow ponies for a man to ride after 'em?"

Banks shook his head and laughed. "Just mustangs. We'll have to trap a few for you. See, we kinda exist out here."

"I savvy *exist*."

"Well if'n you don't know, then you'll learn real quicklike."

"Could I ask what you plan to do with all these wild cattle?"

"We're branding them, making steers out of them, yoking them to gentle them, and plan to get enough to drive them to Sedalia, Missouri, and sell them next year."

Slocum nodded. He'd heard all about what those Bald Knobbers did to Texas cattlemen up there. He'd take his chances catching wild ones and leave the cattle drive to the rest of them.

"We rope them at night when they come out of the brush on these moonlit nights."

Slocum nodded.

"The water barrel is there." Banks gave a head toss toward it on the side of the wagon. "Help yourself. Won't take much to satisfy you. It's only a tad better than hot piss."

"Obliged. Sorry to wake you up."

Banks shook his head to dismiss Slocum's concern. "I can always use another good hand." With his emphasis on *good hand*. "Turn your jackass loose. He won't leave these horses in case you need to ride him out of here later."

"Thanks, my horse foundered a week ago and died."

"Trouble with a good horse. These damn broom-tails we ride, you couldn't kill them short of cutting off their heads and burying them away from their bodies."

"Tough," Slocum agreed.

"So are these cattle. Closer to part deer than anything I've ever seen."

"You a Texan by birth?" Slocum asked, ready to try his first gourd full of the colonel's urine.

Banks acknowledged that, then asked. "You a Georgian?"

Slocum nodded.

"I figured so. Were you an officer?"

"Yes. Captain." Slocum lifted the yellow gourd dipper and slurped in his first mouthful. Hot, wet, and gyp-tasting. The colonel didn't miss the taste.

Banks took out the makings and rolled himself a cigarette, licking it shut with the tip of his tongue. He stuck it in his mouth and held out the makings toward Slocum.

He returned the gourd to its place and took the pouch and papers. "Much obliged."

With an acknowledgment, Banks continued. "Out here we're all enlisted men. I've got the corporal stripes."

"I savvy that." Slocum turned his attention to making

himself a smoke. The notion about having one floated his teeth with a flood of saliva. He'd not had any nicotine in over two weeks. He handed the makings back when he had the cigarette in his lips. With a match he struck with his thumbnail, he fired up. The hot smoke in his lungs at last, he felt the comfort he expected and it set him more at ease.

"We've been lucky—so far." Banks squatted in the shade of the weathered gray wagon and puffed on his roll-your-own. "Ain't had any Injun trouble so far. But that won't hold. Them Comanches're liable to find us and there'll be hell to pay."

"Guess you need to sleep with your gun out here?"

Banks nodded. "I don't figure we'll get this bunch gathered without having some visit by them."

"They've been abducting several kids around the Llano and Mason."

"Dumb damn Krauts anyway. Letting kids herd sheep and goats out there with no one armed to protect them. They're easier than pigeons to pick off."

"They've sent some rangers out there."

Banks shook his head in disgust. "A dozen rangers to cover thousands of acres and there's hundred of them bucks. They'll lose that war worse than we did."

Slocum nodded. He tried not to let the bitterness over the defeat of the Confederacy show on the outside. It was over—his family farm abandoned, a dead carpetbagger judge he'd shot pushing up oxeye daisies, and him on the run from the federal authorities. That summed up his life since Appomattox the year before.

"Can you break your own string?"

"I think so."

"Good. We can trap some tomorrow and then it's up to you. I ain't got a man to spare. You've got ten days to be in the saddle and roping."

"Or after that the food bill starts?"

"Right, then the feed bill starts. In the morning we'll run in a bunch of them mustangs in our trap. There's seven-n-bands around, and then you can pick out the ones you died

Might even get lucky, we've found a few broke ones among them."

"Thanks."

Banks laughed. "You won't ever say that again."

"No, but you'll find I appreciate having a chance."

Banks looked out at the plains distorted by heat waves as if in deep thought and disgust. "Them broncs don't bust you up, roping them longhorns's liable to do it."

Slocum's cigarette finished, he squatted down beside the man in the wagon's half shade from the blazing sun. "I didn't come looking for a job picking roses."

Banks squinted against the sun as if looking at something distant, then shook his head hard in disgust. "That fucking war anyway. I should be home growing cotton and tobacco—not chasing after these bony cattle that once got away from some Spanish conquistador."

"Life deals us all some bad hands."

"Why am I telling you this for—hell, you've got the same story. I had any whiskey left, we'd drink some."

"And I'd toast the better days."

"Fuck, yes."

At supper time, he meet the crew. Paco, a Mexican whose blind eye looked white as a dead fish's. Corky, a thin kid with a pockmarked face and blue eyes that averted looking at anyone. Matt was a hard-jawed fella in his thirties. He wore two guns in cross-draw fashion and his gazes at Slocum spelled suspicion. Hadley was a towhead and grinner in his twenties. He spoke first. "Well, there, Mr. Slocum, mighty fine to have you all here at our little camp meeting." He went on to fill his tin plate while laughing.

"I seen you some'airs before?" Matt asked, giving Slocum a cold cut from his hard eyes as he swept past him.

"I've been lots of places."

"I'll recall it one day," Matt said, going on.

"Buenas tardes, señor," Paco said and nodded to him.

"Gracias, amigo," Slocum said.

"I'm Corky," the kid said. "I do all the dirty jobs. Them rds don't respect or like me."

"That's a shame," Slocum said, and fell in to follow him to the black kettle where they'd been dredging out stew for themselves.

"Yeah, it damn sure is," Corky said over his shoulder, and began to fill his plate with the dipper.

"Ha!" Matt laughed in a taunting fashion from where he sat cross-legged on the ground. "Shut your mouth, you little shit, or I'll notch your other gawdamn ear, kid."

A wary silence filled the late afternoon air. When the kid straightened from filling his plate, Slocum saw the black scab on the kid's right ear and the deep V cut in it.

"You might end up ear-notched yourself," Banks said, coming behind Slocum. "I said any more of that crap, Matt, and you'd answer to me."

"Yes, sir, Colonel," Matt said, and went to shoveling in the chunks of beef and rice with a spoon.

"You better have heard me," Banks said, and went to filling his plate.

Slocum took a couple corn tortillas from the stack and nodded to Lopez, who was standing by observing the others. *"Gracias, hombre."*

A smile parted his gray beard and he showed his white teeth. *"Está bueno."*

"Sí," Slocum said, and went to sit apart from them. He didn't know his allies and enemies amongst this motley crew. There were plenty of rabid killers on the frontier—it paid to learn who they were before one moved into a group. He wasn't there to make friends—he needed the work and the chuck. His belly button had grown to his backbone over the past few months drifting westward. Any work at all was hard to find. Many outfits couldn't afford to even feed you for your efforts, let alone pay you anything for making a hand. He'd split fence rails for his food in east Texas. Worked out his last horse, rounding up some stock after his own mount was stolen one night while he slept. Things in Texas were tough and he regretted leaving Arkansas—but he hoped the dead boy he'd turned into authorities as himself got his name off the federal wanted list. Colby had

of pneumonia up in the Nation and he'd hauled his body down to Van Buren and identified him to the U.S. marshal as John Slocum. Same age, same hair, near the same size and eyes. He'd even collected the fifty-dollar reward—the paper was discounted to thirty-five by a storekeeper in town.

"We'll rope cattle till midnight, then come in tonight," Banks said with the plate of food in his lap. "Dawn, we'll round up some mustangs for Slocum here."

"Yeah, we'll get him some real snuffy ones," Matt said, and laughed at his own words. "You hear me?"

"Snuffy is my kind."

"Glad you ain't deaf yet."

Busy masticating his food, Slocum wasn't being dragged into Matt's conversation. Matt was the kind who looked for a crack he could take offense at and have an outburst over—guns or knives. His species craved drawing blood for any reason or none at all—it fed his ego and thirst, especially doing it to weaker ones like the kid. Slocum would not turn his back on the man.

"You can ride one of Paco's horses tonight," Banks said to him. "I'll get you a *lazo*. We rope them, throw them, and tie their hind legs with the *lazo*. Then they'll be there whenever we go back for them.

"Who needs a lariat besides Slocum?" Banks asked, getting up and dumping his empty plate and utensils in the pail of hot water. No one answered.

Slocum followed him to the wagon. He noticed all the sun-bleached ox yokes in a pile on the ground beside a two-wheel cart—obviously they yoked the cattle up after they caught them to make them gentle.

"Paco's a good hand. He can show you how we catch them," Banks said. "There should be a full moon out tonight. We ought to get several head."

Slocum agreed as the colonel drew the rope off a roll in the wagon, handed him the end, and had him go to a post.

"That's sixty feet," he announced and sliced off the end. "Can you tie a *honda* in the end."

Slocum coiled up the rope as he came back to the wagon. "Never tried. All mine came tied."

"I can show you. But Paco's better at it."

"I'll ask him then."

Banks nodded and spoke under his breath. "This bunch is tough. I don't ask where a man comes from. It won't hurt to keep that in mind."

In the bloody sunset, Slocum could see Paco leading a horse over for him. "Thanks. I've seen what you mean."

"Ah, *mi amigo,* you can ride Estrella." The Mexican gave him the lead.

"That mean Star? He ain't got one in his forehead. Must mean he shoots for the stars."

Paco nodded and grinned. "You want a *honda* braided in the rope?"

"It would help."

"No problema." Paco took the coil and tucked it under his arm as they walked the horse back to Slocum's gear. Paco's deft brown fingers began to open a twist about six inches from the end. Next, he frayed that part and braided it in the opening. With a large pig-sticker from his boot, he trimmed off the fuzzy tails.

"Now, amigo, we need some wax so the rope will slide through it." Paco walked to the wagon, came back to him with a candle and the lariat still clamped under his arm. "Light it and we will drizzle the hot wax on the *honda.*"

The operation only required minutes, and he used his thumb to rub it in the rope. "There's one fine lariat."

"Gracias," Slocum said, and took it from him.

"You ever rope spooks before?"

"No."

"These gringos, they rope tied hard and fast—" He shook his head in disapproval. "You don't want that sometimes. I dally-rope, then when it gets too hot, you can toss the rope to them and ride out of the way."

"I savvy dally. Keep your fingers out of it." Slocum tossed his pads on the bay, then the saddle. He walked around to let out the latigos drawn up to fit Judas, and Paco came on the other side to help him.

"Better to lose a finger than your life. We have buried three men out here so far."

"I figured this was a tough business," Slocum said. "How many steers can you rope in a month?"

"I rope two or more a night if we can find them."

Slocum nodded and moved around to cinch the horse up. It would be twilight in another few minutes. At that rate, he could make some pocket change once he had his own string of horses broke to ride. Better learn all he could on this trip; they didn't give second lessons in these outfits—but Paco sounded all right.

"*Gracias,*" Slocum said as the man went for his own horse.

Paco waved that he'd heard him and swung in the saddle. "Let's ride. We need to go down by the big thicket."

"Bet you that I get more than you boys do tonight," Matt said, riding past them in a long trot.

"I bet you two bits," Paco said.

"Hell, make it worth my while," Matt whined.

"No more, hombre."

"I'll take your two bits—the night I can't outrope a spic, I'll quit." Matt put spurs to his horse and it started off in two crow hops and then began to run.

"Braggart. I beat him all the time and he never quits gouging me," Paco said after him. "I wish he would quit."

Slocum and Paco sat on a ridge. Their ponies were hip-shot as Slocum studied the gloomy dark thicket that stretched for miles back to the east. Below them, the silver light shone on the knee-high greasewood sea emitting a smell of creosote on the night wind.

Slocum rubbed his calloused palm over his mouth. Somewhere a coyote yipped and a big male answered with a throaty howl. They were out for the white-tailed deer that hid in the brush—soon one in the pack would find a fresh scent and they'd take off yapping and howling, sending chills up the spine of the does with their fawns about to be weaned.

Like two coyotes, he and Paco waited for their prey to emerge. It would be a real long night with little rest. He could only hope the upsurge of excitement would keep him awake enough to do this job.

"There," Paco whispered and pointed. The dark shadows of the head-tossing cattle began to emerge from the black forest. Pausing to graze here and there, they went westward swishing their tails. The leader raised his six-foot horn span and paused to sniff the night air, but Slocum and Paco were downwind of them. Then the bunch marched on, snatching grass as they went across the open land, soon followed by others.

No shortage of cattle this night. Slocum felt the weight of the two *lazos* strung around his neck. Maybe he could fill some before midnight.

Paco held out his hand. "Not yet, *mi amigo*. We want them far away from the brush because once we chase them, they will head back for it."

Slocum acknowledged his words. His stomach churned. In his heart, he hoped he was up to the test. He damn sure needed this job.

2

They shook loose their lariats and rode as quietly as they could downhill. Slocum knew once they struck the cattle's trail, they'd have to ride full tilt to ever get a rope on them. He stood in the stirrups to see better in the silver light and ease the jarring of the trot.

"Rope it, then ride past it and throw the rope over its rump. Then you ride sideways and bust it on the ground. Once it's down you must dismount, run over, and tie the hind legs fast, savvy?"

"Savvy."

"Let's vamoose," Paco said, and they were off in hot pursuit.

The longhorn silhouettes threw their horns in the air and flushed.

"I got the one on my side," Slocum said, feeding out rope to make a larger loop. Damn, his horns looked ten feet wide. Standing in his stirrups, guiding Star with one hand, he began to whirl the lariat over his head. Near the hard-running critter's butt, he reached out and tossed the loop over one horn and the head. Good enough—he made the dally around the saddle horn and turned Star off in a sweeping arc to the left. The rope cut into the top of his leg when the steer hit the end and it about jerked Star over backward. The pony

11

kept digging in, and Slocum slipped off his back and ran to the downed steer. In seconds, he had its hind feet tied and his first wild cattle catch was complete.

His heart beating rapidly, he took his lariat off the head-slinging critter as it flopped on the ground bawling its head off in protest—because with its hind legs tied it couldn't get up.

On the run, Slocum coiled his rope as he headed back for Star, coaxing the loose horse not to run from him as he approached. The pony acted spooked, but Slocum finally caught a rein and was on board again. They left in a flurry. Paco was nowhere in sight on the silver sea. Slocum spotted a single longhorn in a long trot headed back for the thicket.

He set spurs to Star and the pony headed for the critter. In a dead run, Star stumbled once, but scrambled and quickly recovered his footing. With the greasewood whipping Slocum's legs, he wished for chaps, but urged the gelding on faster, building a new loop as they flew over the flat and closed in on the galloping bovine.

Up in the stirrups so his weight was over Star's front end as he lunged forward to catch their prey, Slocum whistled the lariat over his head and then threw it. The catch was good. He jerked his slack, cinching the rope around half of the critter's head and horn; then he dallied on the saddle and turned Star to the side.

In an instant, he felt the pony lose his footing and stumble. Slocum managed to hold his dally and step down as the rope went tight. Star fell on his side and the maverick went flying on the other end. No time to check on the horse. Slocum sped on his boots though the brittle greasewood. Before the stunned critter could get up, he leaped on its thrashing hindquarters, which were seeking traction, and hitched the *lazo* around its heels before he could recover.

Out of breath and in a sweat, he sat for a moment on the bawling critter's rump and drew in some night air. Fifty feet away in the moonlight, Star was on his feet, rattling the stirrups as he shook himself in a cloud of dust. Maybe the pony was all right. Slocum was out of *lazos* and there was still time to rope some more. Coiling his lariat, he headed for Star. Better go find Paco.

When he rode Star off, the cow pony felt sound under him, and Slocum pushed his hat back to thank the heavens one more time for his good fortune. He stood in the stirrups as they headed westerly searching the landscape for any sign of a horse and rider. Several determined-acting cattle skirted him headed in a long trot for the thicket. Their great horns shone in the starlight.

He rode past a bawling tied-up maverick, obviously the work of Paco. Digging up dust with its right horn and propelling itself around in a circle on the ground, the critter made plenty of dust.

Over the next rise, Slocum spotted the rider under the sombrero-shaped hat closing in on another one. The catch made, Paco's horse swung left and the steer went ass over teakettle in the air. Paco ran for him and shouted *"Viva!"* after he tied him.

"Ah, you get one?" Paco asked, coiling his rope.

Slocum caught his horse and led him back. "Two. I'm out of ties."

"Two? Man, you are a real vaquero. I will have to work hard to beat you."

"Beginner's luck. I need another *lazo*. They're all headed for the brush." He nodded behind them, and caught the short rope that Paco tossed to him.

They charged over the flats, hoping to find more cattle before they escaped into the thicket.

"There!" Paco shouted as two head split in front of them; one went to Slocum's side, the other to Paco's. Standing in the stirrups, Slocum shook loose his rope and urged Star on. The ground they crossed made a rise that slowed the steer, and then the animal tried to cut back toward the other steer. Without a choice, Slocum roped him off-handed and gave him some slack before he dallied to give Star a chance to get his feet under him.

The longhorn stopped with a hard jerk on the end. Slocum bailed the pony right at him. Screaming like a banshee to make him run aside instead of charging them, Slocum tossed the slack over his hip and then sent Star sideways. His action flipped the steer in the air. In a flash, Slocum was out of the saddle and running to make it number three. Out of breath on his knees beside his prey, he jerked his tie rope tight and fell backward on his butt to avoid the two kicking hooves. That made three.

"Get some good horses and you will beat my record," Paco said, riding up, coiling his rope. "We better get back or we won't get no sleep."

"And I damn sure need some." Slocum bounced off his toes into the saddle and reined Star around. One thing for certain, he'd have a tough time repeating his score on green horses.

The colonel took the tally when they came into camp.

"Six," Paco said. "Me and him."

"Damn, you boys done all right."

"How many Matt get?"

"He ain't in yet."

Paco turned in the saddle to look into the night for him. "He will do anything to beat me."

"Nice job, Slocum," Banks said.

"I got lucky."

"Luck must trail you then." Banks laughed.

"How many did them others catch?" Paco asked, dropping heavily from the saddle with a crash of his spur rowels.

"Three between them."

"We'll need a new place tonight. Those *vacas* get plenty smart about us."

"Yeah," Banks agreed. "We need some tiger dogs to bay them."

Slocum stopped unsaddling. "What's that?"

"Them folks in east Texas use brindle dogs that tree them. I tried to buy some before we came out here. They won't even sell me a pup."

"I'll remember that. Brindle dogs that tree cattle." He'd never heard of them.

"Sunup we roll out," Banks reminded them as they dragged off to their bedrolls.

Later, on the ground in his bedding set aside from the others, Slocum listened to the insects creaking. Good to have found work—tough bunch, but he'd survived tougher ones. His thoughts went back to the good-looking, naked women he could recall, and he rolled over on his side, a little disappointed there wasn't one in his blankets to share the rising erection.

3

They located a band of wild horses and Banks gave the riders their orders, sending them to encircle the bunch so the mustangs were forced to flee into the trap. Riding a dun horse that belonged in Hadley's string, Slocum slid it off a loose bank into a dry wash, waving his coil of rope and shouting to turn some undecided horses toward the pen. The aggregate of man and beast boiled up lots of dust that rose high into the sky, and a lack of wind did little to dissipate it. Everyone pulled up their kerchiefs to filter it out, and fought hard to turn back the suspicious mustangs into the pen. Horses broke right—thwarted, they tried left, but the loop drawn in by the riders soon cut off any exit and they thundered into the large trap.

Corky ran up and dragged the gate closed.

In the suspended dust, the crew reined up with only their eyes not floured by the tan-gray dust.

"Go get some sleep. They're his now," Banks shouted, and turned his horse toward camp.

Slocum nodded, dismounted, and tied the dun to a post. He went and found a place in the meager lacy shade of a mesquite, and sat cross-legged on the ground. No reason to try and go into that pen yet; let them churn around until the afternoon wind came up. That would clear the dust out so he could see what he had. Twenty, thirty head, some mares and colts to cut out, maybe a stud, but he'd not seen or heard one.

If the right stallion was in there, he might just cut him and ride him. Late-cut horses made powerful mounts, with more muscle than a fantailed gelding castrated as a yearling and turned out. Of course, that depended on whether the horse survived the surgery. Cattle were no problem to neuter— horses required some skills. Especially castrating older ones. His curiosity aroused, Slocum wondered about his new cavvy and how breaking them would go.

He didn't have long to wait. The rising hot wind soon swept the dust cloud away. He leaned his arms on the gate and looked the bunch over. Four mares with colts, and the rest were older horses. Two geldings bore saddle sores and looked gaunt. He led the dun into the pen, mounted up, and roped one.

The first captured pony acted a little spooky. One white sock, and he wore a Diamond A brand on his right shoulder. When Slocum rode in and made a halter on his head, he calmed some. He was smooth-mouthed, but solid enough— obviously the horse had been born before the war and been broken. Maybe stolen by raiding Comanche and had escaped them. Slocum decided to try him. He hobbled the dun and tossed his pack on the new bay—christened him Diamond as he cinched him up. He acted like it had been a while since he'd been handled, but Slocum ignored the fact. Too much to do and too little time to do it.

He cheeked Diamond from his head to his leg and piled on. With both Slocum's feet in the stirrups, Diamond bogged his nose between his knees. He bucked across the pen and back before Slocum wrenched his head up and forced him to lope in tight circles. Then he set spurs to Diamond and charged him hard across the pen, sliding him to a hard halt. Diamond would do. *Numero uno*—good.

He used Diamond to catch the horse with white gall marks on his withers. Another tall gelding that could use a hundred or more pounds on him. A bay with no markings, he bore some scars on his chest. The brand had been a hair one and was closed over, but Slocum traced it with his finger—a

U. His cow-kicking, squealing pony became Ute after Slocum mouthed him—ten to twelve years old, but sound enough. He'd break him of that cow-kicking quicklike if he had to wear a boot toe out kicking his belly.

Slocum used a rope around the horse's neck, and then with the other end pulled his hind foot up and tied it, so if he dared kick he'd become unbalanced and fall over. Saddle in place, Slocum used a sack on him to get the spook out of him. With his foot up, all Ute could do was flinch uncomfortably, until he finally stopped worrying about the sack being waved and slapped at him.

There was water in the trap so the horses could stay there for a day or so until Slocum got his string cut out. Then Slocum saw him—looking square at the big blue roan with the long tangling black mane that concealed his eyes. The stud—a real bulldog of a horse, broad and stout. He pawed his right hoof in the dust and squealed out of his nose in defiance. *You'll do just fine.*

Two broke horses and there were two others that acted sound, but carried no brands. A high-headed pacer that looked like a dirty buckskin, and a shorter big-eyed chestnut. Both needed cut. So if Slocum had three to geld—he'd not get much roping done with them till they healed. Take them a while too, so that they'd be sore enough to break some easier. He'd talk to Paco about doing the job—if anyone was a hand at it, the Mexican might be.

He worked the mares, colts, and yearlings out of the pen. So by late afternoon he had it down to his own bunch and rode Diamond, leading his borrowed pony. At camp he hobbled Diamond and turned him out—be a while before he trusted the gelding to stay around.

He washed his sun-heated face and hands in the basin set out, dried them on a stiff sack, then headed for the stew.

"Kinda showing off, ain't yah?" Matt said, sitting on the ground wolfing down his supper. "Riding in on a bronc."

"Two broke horses in that bunch," Slocum said and nodded to Lopez, who never said much.

"Hell, I wanted to see you get your ass busted," Matt said.

"Don't run off. You still may." Slocum took some of the corn tortillas to put on top of his stew and thanked the old man.

"I ain't leaving," Matt blurted out. "Gawdamnit, Corky, you're so fucking ugly, the damn doctor probably slapped your mother for having you."

"Go to hell."

"I'll send your ass there if you don't shut up."

"You ain't my boss."

Slocum wondered where the colonel was at. He didn't let Matt pick on anyone like that when he was around. Matt was trying to rowel the kid up into a gunfight—a grossly one-sided event if it unfolded.

"Matt that kid ain't bothered you," Hadley said.

"Yes, he has."

"Colonel Banks ain't going to stand for you running roughshod over the crew."

A sly smile crept over Matt's whisker-bristled face, his eyes gleamed with pleasure. "I can send both of you to hell—"

The click of a shotgun hammer shut him up. Then the soft, accented voice of Lopez behind the stock said, "Nobody is going to hell but you."

"Listen, you old greaser, you better pull that trigger or I'm cutting your balls off."

"Get your stuff and ride out of *cheer*," Lopez said.

Slocum watched the scene unfold. The old man was serious, and Slocum had no doubts Lopez'd blow daylight through the gunman if he tried anything.

"Banks owes me—"

"No. Señor—you have forfeited that money."

"Like hell—"

"You want to live or me to put the money in your grave?"

"All right, but I ever catch you away from the damn gun—I'll—"

"Go! Go now!"

Matt looked the bunch over. All the crew was standing, each one with a hand on his gun butt, and by the looks that Slocum saw on their faces—Matt was outnumbered. He might have been surly, but against those odds, he swept up his pack and went for a horse. He cursed under his breath and made plenty of threats, but in the sundown's red glare he rode out promising to get all of them.

Slocum shared a nod of approval with Lopez. Good riddance.

At dawn, when the crew came in from a night of roping, they stretched out the three horses on the ground between two ropers; then, one at a time, Paco stole their seeds in the deft manner that Slocum had expected. He tied Judas halter to halter with the chestnut. The sassy burro would teach him to lead shortly. By purchasing some grain from the colonel to feed his two broke horses, Slocum could use them every other day while his other mounts healed. Hobbled, the newfound geldings mostly stood around downcast and sore from the surgery. But each morning when he returned from cow chasing, he'd saddle one and tie up a hind foot. Then, at night, he'd hobble that one and let it go to water.

Slocum averaged over two steers a night. The entire crew acted different with Matt gone. They laughed and joked at meals. The atmosphere was better—like relief had set in.

One evening after Slocum had switched the saddle off the roan, the colonel was in a talkative mood at the washbasin.

"Should have run Matt off a long time ago. We're getting as many cattle as we did with him here. Maybe more."

"How's the tally?" Slocum asked.

"We have close to eight hundred." He talked soft so their conversation was private at the back of the wagon.

Slocum nodded.

"While I was gone to get more yokes from that Mexican and some supplies, I raised a little money. There's a couple of ugly whores south of here at a small community called Rio Frio and they've got some pulque to drink. Maybe we all ought to go down there and celebrate?"

"You mean the whole crew?"

"Sure, they've all been working hard. Move our camp to the lunar lake south of here tonight and the horses will have feed and water. We can be gone a day and night and then ride back."

"Fine with me."

"A little pussy won't hurt anyone." The colonel laughed and clapped Slocum on the shoulder in a puff of dust. "Might double the number they catch when they get back."

"All of us going?" Slocum asked.

"Naw. Lopez can watch things. He ain't horny as the rest of us."

"I'm ready."

"Crew, listen up, we're moving camp and sleeping tonight. We've got the steers all yoked you caught last night. Let's move down to that moon lake and then we'll ride into Rio Frio. The drinks and whores will be on me."

"EEHA!" Hats flew in the air. Hadley busted a few caps in his pistol and locked arms with Corky in an Irish jig.

So, after the two-wheel cart half full of the crude yokes was hitched to two oxen, four saddle horses were harnessed and hitched, and all of Lopez's camp stuff was stowed in the wagon, they set out in the starlight for the moon lake, a body of water without an outlet to its depression. Most lakes were shallow and dried up by late summer; others held liquid due to some recent cloudburst on the watershed-covered acres. This one, Slocum felt, would last them a while, and it attracted the wild cattle too.

Under the stars, they reached the new site and set things up in a party mood. It was past midnight when they fell in their bedrolls acting excited as little kids the night before Christmas.

For breakfast, Lopez cooked his usual frijoles and beef. The crew was covered with dirt as they wolfed down their food and went to saddle horses. Except for his hands and face, Slocum felt top-dressed in his west Texas dirt. His clothes, stiff with his sweat, had turned to adobe. He wet his lips and swung on Diamond. *What the hell anyway?*

When he came back, he promised himself he would ride the roan horse. That might be a handful even in the horse's depressed mood from surgery. He was still proud and when

Slocum had saddled him, he'd acted plenty tough. Threatening to bite or kick Slocum, his small ears laid back, he'd be a handful, but as Slocum jogged Diamond after the others— he sort of looked forward to it. About as much as he did thinking about the *putas* ahead. Whew, they better be ready—this bunch carried enough pecker power to awe a big flock of sheep.

"What's so funny?" Hadley asked, moving in, obviously seeing the smile on Slocum's sun-crusted lips.

"I imagined a flock of sheep stampeding at the sight of this horny bunch."

Hadley slapped his chap-covered leg and agreed. "We may use 'em up."

Dust churned up by their horses soon forced them to fan out in a line. It was a few hours before Slocum could see several distorted jacales through the heat waves. He pointed them out. They looked like a mirage on the southern horizon.

"That it, Colonel?" Corky asked.

Banks nodded. "That's where it was last week."

"Geez, I can't wait—"

"You better wait till you get it in her," Paco teased.

"I screwed a French girl in Orleans," Corky said, looking starry-eyed from under his floppy straw hat. "Man, it was like screwing a mink. She was all over that bed and room."

"Aw, yes, the high-yellow whores of the French Quarter are like butterflies with teeth." The colonel laughed and threw his head back. "These *putas* ain't that lively." Then he snickered out his nose. "I damn near married one of the finest New Orleans whores in town—'cept I kept remembering my old daddy's words. 'Fuck 'em, son, but don't never get plumb attached. They ain't your kind.' "

They dismounted in a row in front of the adobe structure with faded letters on the wall—CANTINA. His horse hitched, Slocum loosened the cinch and looked around. He'd have someone feed it some grain—he about had the two broke horses in rock-hard shape. Grain for the two cost twenty cents, but he easily made that up catching cattle.

"EEHA!" the kid shouted, and parted the old batwing doors with both hands to enter. "I'm horny as a grizzly bear and twice as thirsty."

"Ah, come in, Señor. I have plenty pulque and many fine ladies."

"How many whores you got?" The kid blocked the door like he might turn away if the answer didn't suit him.

"Three." The bartender held up his fingers.

"Aw, hell, I can screw that many and want more myself." The kid dropped his chin crestfallen. "But—I'll share 'em. Come on in, boys." Corky waved them on. "The pulque and pussy is on the boss."

"Cinco hombres?" The bartender set five mugs on the bar and looked for the answer.

When the kid nodded, the barman said, "Dis is on me."

"Very generous," the kid said, and waited as the man poured the yellowish slurry in each one, a cheap version of thick Mexican beer fermented from corn.

"What's your name?" the kid asked.

"Ah, Dialgo."

"Good. Dialgo, I'm toasting the colonel." Corky raised his mug and the others joined him. "Hurrah to the colonel."

"Yes," said the others.

Mug in his hand, Slocum had noticed the dust-coated trophy deer head over the back bar. There were also a large smoky mirror and a near-life-size painting of two chunky nudes with the devil himself finger-fucking one of them with her legs spread wide apart, the second one fondling his large erection with a look that said she might soon eat it.

Enter the three *putas*—a wide-hipped and short one led the charge through the curtain from the back room. "Ah, Chihuahua, the vaqueros are here, girls."

"Yes!" the other two screamed like schoolgirls, jumping up and down.

Corky, with foam on his fuzzy upper lip, swept over and squeezed her around the waist. "You ready to fuck?"

"Sí." Her dark eyes flashed with excitement.

"Get on the table."

"Oh, no!" She looked offended at the very idea.

"Oh, yes," he said and stripped down his suspenders.

Impatient with her disobeying him, he took her by the waist and put her on the table, then unbuttoned his pants. Soon he held a long pink dick in his fist, throwing her dress back and scooting her to the edge. He pushed her down on the top of the table, gathered her brown legs, and waded between the short sausage-shaped limbs to insert his dick in her cunt with a hard plunge forward of his hatchet ass.

She cried like it was too big, and everyone laughed. The race was on. Her heels around his neck, he was hard-humping her pale brown ass. His breath raged in and out. He continued on and on to the cheers of the crowd. "Fuck her, kid!"

Then his butt hunched in a final drive and he stepped in gathering her hard toward him. He gave a short grunt, a hard hunch into her, and then his face paled. He staggered back and shook his head looking around bleary-eyed. "Who's next?"

The colonel clapped him on the shoulder. "Better have a drink and share them."

"Thank you, sir, but I'm just getting started."

"We've got all day and all night."

"I guess so," he said, tucking his still-half-hard dick in his pants. "You know, Colonel, that was about as good as that New Orleans stuff."

Hadley stepped over and took the wide-hipped one by the hand when she slipped off the table. She smiled at him like a cat about to eat a large fish, and took him quickly through the curtain into the back. No more tabletop fucking for her.

The short one in her teens, Lenora, came over and inspected Slocum and Paco. "Toss a coin, *mis amigos*. Winner gets me first."

Paco flipped a small gold coin in the air and slapped it on the bar.

"Heads," Slocum said.

Paco nodded with a smile. "You win her."

"Come," she said before Slocum changed his mind. She dragged him past the colonel, Corky, and a whore called Farita who were drinking the sour pulque.

Down the hall, Lenora took Slocum into her sweltering room. The sunshine shone in the high window and sprayed the dull room with golden light. She cleared the blouse off her head and exposed her small breasts topped with pointed dark nipples, while he toed off his boots. Then she unlaced her skirt and wiggled out of it with a grin. Under her tits, her belly made a slight bow, disappearing over the thatch of black pubic hair.

He dropped his suspenders and unbuttoned his shirt. Then he pulled the kerchief off, handing it and his hat to her. She held the hat over the V where her legs met and smiled at him.

"You like me?"

"Oh, yes." Hell, he'd like a bucktooth goat at this point.

She hung his hat on a peg, then came and undid his pants, spreading them open so they fell to his knees. Then she cradled his scrotum in her palm and kissed the hairy top of his flat belly. Crowded against him so her hard nipples nailed his skin, she used both hands to carefully roll his nuts around, forcing him to stand on his toes.

"I am too rough?" she asked with a mischievous grin.

"No," he gasped, short of wind, and hunched himself toward her as his erection in the form of a limber fishing pole began to rise and stiffen.

Her hungry mouth played on his chest as she continued to massage his testicles. Then she knelt down on her knees and used the tip of her tongue to taste the head of his dick on the underside. Catlike, she licked on it first, then encircled the expanding head with her fiery mouth. Her actions sent electricity like lightning up his spine. He clutched his fingers in her thick hair and brought her head toward him. Then, with fury, she began to suck on it, swallowing more of the length with each charge.

At last, with spittle and fluids running from the corners of her mouth, she gasped, "The bed," and dove on it.

In an instant, she was on her back with her legs spread

apart. She pulled him down on top of her—crawfishing under him to insert his aching iron rod in her gates. With an arch of her back, she cried out in pleasure when he began to probe her. His swollen organ filled the gap and the walls contracted in spasms as he pumped in and out of her. He ground his pubic bone on hers, and the coarse hair felt on fire from the friction. The tip of his dick was ready to explode. He looked down as she tossed her head and heavy curls on the sheet, crying, "Mother of God! *Está muy grande!*"

She wrapped her small legs around the back of his and hunched to him in rabbit fashion until her large clitoris grew rock-hard under his dick's action. Then she threw her arms out and gasped. He felt his own charge gain momentum to fly out of his scrotum, and when he came, she clutched his arms so tight it hurt.

He could feel the waves of tremors in her belly underneath his own, and he strained hard, drove himself deep as he could go in her. This time, in both sides of his ass, hot needles shot into him and he closed his eyes as he braced above her and came again. *Whew, what a lay. Who said them French whores were so good? Oh, Lenora, you wonderful angel.*

4

The next day, hungover and his balls as sore as his dick, he rode Diamond home with the rest of the aching heads. He glanced back once or twice to see the heat-wave-distorted ja-cales and wonder about the young *puta* Lenora—not a real pretty girl. Her nose was too thick and her lower lip too fat. He'd known lots of better bodies, but few who could screw like that—with meaning. It was her big eyes, and thick hair to run his fingers through and clutch, that he remembered most. Then her groaning even when he later used his finger to play with her huge clit. A heavenly angel among the dried bunch-grass, mesquite, greasewood, pear-cactus beds, and gyp wa-ter of west Texas. He could still taste and smell her musk above his own sweat and Diamond's.

"Slocum, we need to start taking the yokes off those first steers we worked six weeks ago or so. I intend to drive them all up to Mason and winter them there till grass breaks out," the colonel said as they jog-trotted northward. "In the morning, you and Paco can take some supplies and horses and ride back up north. Start collecting the steers and get-ting the yokes off. I want to save all of them damn yokes I can, so pile them up on the wagon tracks and we'll collect them going out. I may need a second cart to haul all of them."

"You taking the herd to Mason when we get them shaped up?"

The colonel nodded. "I've got a place up there with some grass and water to hold 'em."

Slocum moved in close. "What're they worth in Missouri?"

"Eight, ten cents a pound at Sedalia, last I heard."

"That would kill a hundred dollars for each head."

"Yeah, but it's risky damn business and catching them ain't cheap."

Slocum agreed—nothing was easy. He lifted the reins to check Diamond to match Bank's horse's gait. With eight hundred to a thousand head of steers up there, he was talking thousands of dollars. No wonder they ran the risk of Bald Knobbers and hillbilly rustlers while getting to the railhead. If a man ever made it there, his days would be easy from then on.

Banks rocked his saddle with his hand on the horn as they rode on. "I figure I can buy a damn fancy place for that kinda money."

"Why, sure, I'd hope to hell you can."

"I've got to get them to market first."

Slocum nodded in agreement. "Man's got dreams, he needs to fill 'em."

"What about you? You got any dreams."

Slocum shook his head. "All in my pipe. I guess they have gone up in smoke."

"Something will show up." Banks nodded like he was convinced it would happen.

"We'll see. Thanks."

The colonel frowned at him. "Your're always so damn grateful."

"I told you my navel was gouging my spine when I hired on with you."

Banks laughed. "It was my good fortune."

Lopez had supper in the pot when they rode in. Brown beans and beef—he must have tired of his rice and beef, Slocum decided. He still took several corn tortillas and went to find him a place to sit on the ground. His personal mustangs had raised their heads up from grazing when they rode in the night before—they looked about recovered from the cutting. He'd need to take a couple along and break them out unyoking and bunching cattle for the colonel.

Before the sun showed more than a purple smile on the eastern horizon, he and Paco left camp, each with a repeating Spencer rifle and several tubes of cartridges the colonel had issued them. Just in case. Slocum took Roan, Diamond, Pacer—the dirty-colored buckskin, and rode Ute. His pack was on Diamond. Paco was outfitted with four head—one to ride and one to pack and two on the lead. Slocum led the string and Paco kept them trotting with a quirt. They hustled over the greasewood sea, and held up past noon to eat some pepper-jerky at a spring that Paco knew about.

They squatted on their boot heels and chewed the leather-tough jerky that Lopez had made from some critter that broke a leg or neck in the roping. Suddenly, the horses saw something and jerked their heads up looking east—a warning. Slocum's hand went for his gun butt.

"Could be a coyote," Paco said with his gun hand on the handle also.

"Could be a Comanche too." Slocum rose slowly trying to see in the scattered mesquite for sign of any movement.

"To the right." Paco pointed at a hatless figure wrapped in a blanket running low and away from them down the draw.

"Watch the horses." Slocum picked up Ute's trailing reins and vaulted into the saddle.

"It could be a trap too!" Paco shouted after him.

"I'll see," Slocum said. He wanted to cut the figure off before he reached any others. Then, perhaps Slocum could learn his business and how many more were around there. Ute was ducking the bigger mesquites, switching leads left and right in a hard run after the fleeing figure. Still, branches were slapping Slocum's face as he bore down on the hard-running individual. Leaning low on Ute's neck, he reached out and caught a fistful of blanket. Sliding Ute to a hard stop on his butt, he hauled the empty blanket over his lap in disgust—he'd lost the figure he was pursuing.

Then he twisted in the saddle and blinked twice in shock at what he saw. A stark-naked white woman stood with her arms folded over her pear-shaped breasts and looking defiantly at him. A young woman in her early twenties with a shapely body who looked angry as hell at him and modest about her exposure. What was she doing out there in only an Indian trade blanket? Damn. He reined Ute around and rode back holding the blanket out as a peace offering like some sheep-killing dog.

"Sorry, I thought you were a buck out to lift my scalp."

She took the blanket, shook it out, and when it covered her nakedness, struck a dignified pose. "My name is Mary Van Housen."

"Nice to meet you, ma'am." Slocum removed his hat as he introduced himself to her.

"I am going to Fredricksburg, Mr. Slocum," she said like someone on a stroll.

He acknowledged he'd heard her, but he was afraid she had no idea how far away it was.

"Do you live there?" he asked.

"I did until they made me a captive."

"You have any family there?"

"No. They shot my husband. Murdered my baby boy because he cried—"

"Sorry, ma'am."

"And I—and I—was repeatedly raped by them." Her eyes looked sad and she raised her chin with a sniff to hold back the tears.

"I'm sorry about that too. How did you get away?" He slipped off his horse and squatted on his heels, not looking at her so she wouldn't feel conspicuous.

"My captors were six boys—just boys—maybe fifteen—fourteen. I think it was their first attack on anyone. It was on our farm. They took me and Billy prisoner after they shot and—scalped John. It was very upsetting—I couldn't get my two-year-old to stop crying—they killed him after they lost two of their own to a group of men who began firing on us for no reason.

"I had hoped at first they were rangers, but they went crazy at the sight of the war party and began shooting like mad. Bullets whizzed all over and around us. One struck the horse they had put me on—but he turned out all right. Only a shallow wound. Two of the boys were dead, though, and the other four mad as hornets. I even thought they'd kill me for a while."

"You were lucky."

"They took all my clothing so I wouldn't run away. I was forced to accept them—" She looked ready to cry again and bit her lower lip. "Two nights ago I stole a blanket and a horse and rode away."

"Where's the horse?"

"He got afraid of a rattler that struck at him and I slipped off his back to calm him. But he had a head-slinging fit, pulled away, and ran off with his tail held high and headed back for his Comanche friends, I guess."

"Ma'am, Paco and me are working for a man gathering his cattle. It's our job, but you could come along and later this fall someone could take you home."

Lines wrinkled her smooth forehead. "How far away is Fredricksburg?"

"Couple hundred miles, I'd guess."

"Oh," she said in pained defeat. "I thought it was only a few more."

"No, it's several days ride from out here."

"But I have no clothes—" She sighed in defeat.

"I've got a spare shirt that would make you a short dress—" He nodded, appraising her size. "Should come below your knees, and later I promise we can find something else in a town close by."

He rose with a ringing of his spurs and went over to his saddlebags. The white dress shirt he'd saved for something special was wadded up; he tossed it at her and kept his back to her while she put it on.

Without turning, he asked, "How's that?"

"Oh, you can look now." She finished buttoning the front, and it reached below her knees when she straightened. "Thanks, I feel much better."

"Little big in the shoulders." He laughed, and she smiled back.

"I've been without clothes for several weeks. This shirt makes me feel, oh, so much better, but it'll soon be dirty."

"It can be washed." He swept up her blanket and handed it to her. "Paco may think I'm dead. Let's go find him."

"What's he like?"

"A solid, one-eyed Mexican fellow. You'll like him."

He swung in the saddle and then bent over offering her his arm. She hugged it and he set her on behind him. "Keep your heels out of his flank. He's goosey enough without that."

At his back, she squirmed to get in place, and her hands were on his hips for balance as she settled in. Looking down and seeing her fine, shapely, snowy legs beside his dirty canvas pants on both sides, he booted Ute off to find Paco.

He rode up to the frowning Mexican and swung her down. "Paco, meet Señora Van Housen."

Paco swept off his big sombrero and bowed for her with a laugh. "I send him after Comanche and he brings back a wonderfully beautiful lady—good day, Señora."

"Nice to meet you, Mr. Paco. My name is Mary. Señor Slocum has offered me your protection until someone is going to my home."

"Oh, I am only Paco. But you are very welcome in our camp."

Slocum handed her the blanket and dismounted. "She's been running from them for several days with only a blanket to wear. The horse she stole from them got away from her."

Paco looked saddened at her pain. "I am so sorry, Mary."

She raised her chin. "I'm alive. God looked after me. I am prepared to return to my people."

"We need to make camp here tonight. We're about a day's ride from the north end of our operation," Paco said to Slocum.

"Looks fine to me."

"What's your job here?" she asked Slocum.

"Unyoking wild cattle. The cowboys catch them, brand

and work them, then put them in yokes. It gentles them down."

"Sometimes." Paco laughed and shook his head in disbelief. "Nothing is easy out here."

Slocum agreed, and undid the diamond hitch over the pack. She moved in to help him, pulling off the tarp covering.

"I could almost cry. Finding two strong men in the middle of—" She looked around and wet her lips. "Nowhere."

"No need to cry. We're just some ranch hands."

She whirled and looked hard at him. "No, you are my angels."

"How long since you ate anything?" Slocum asked.

She shook her head. "I don't recall."

"That's what I thought. You're delirious from lack of nourishment."

Her sunbaked forehead wrinkled. "No, I'm not."

"No, but I bet you can eat."

"Oh, yes. Anytime. A few weeks with *them* and you eat whenever you get a chance as well as whatever there is available, which sometimes is extremely disgusting."

"I bet so. Paco's dragging in more deadwood. I better start a fire or we won't ever eat."

"I can do that. You have a match?"

"One?"

"One will do if it will light."

"Take two," he said, and went to busting up sticks into kindling with his hands.

The fire was soon under way, and she began to chunk up the back strip of beef that Lopez' had sent along. A fresh enough kill—it shouldn't have spoiled—wrapped all day in a wet flour sack to keep it cool.

When the fire got hot, she browned the chunks in the small iron kettle, then set them aside. She put water in the kettle and set it to boil for the brown rice. Slocum saw she was proficient enough at cooking, so he went and tossed his saddle and pads on the foot-stomping roan. With its hind foot drawn up, all the roan could do was act tough and shake his long thick mane in defiance.

After the saddling, Slocum left the gear on to condition him to it. He and Paco went back and squatted away from the fire. She'd made some dough, and handed them long forked sticks.

"Want some bread?" she asked.

"Sure," Slocum said and moved in. Taking the dough ball she gave him, he put it on the stick and began to hold it over the fire.

Soon, Paco joined him, laughing. "I am sure glad, *mi amigo,* that you found her. I dreaded our cooking all day coming up here."

Slocum agreed. In a few minutes, the bread on his stick was brown. He offered her half of his because she was busy stirring the rice. She set the spoon aside and took a chunk and tossed it in her hands. "Still hot."

He agreed, and rearmed his stick to bake more while he ate his half. As he nibbled on the fresh warm bread, saliva rushed into his mouth. Her involvement in camp routine left him time to study her. Attractive, with long dark lashes that sheltered large brown pools that showed her emotions and pleasure—perhaps her gratefulness to be in their care. Her mouth looked made to kiss with a rose petal for a lower lip. Not tall—she might be all of five feet two in her bare feet— with thick curly dark brown hair that fell to her collar and, despite her abuse and captivity, looked glossy.

Her figure he could imagine under the too-big shirt, from what he'd seen when she was naked earlier. A slender waist, with shapely legs under the black V at the base of her flat stomach, and the pear-shaped breasts that poked dark circles on the shirt material. Seated cross-legged opposite the fire from her, he could only imagine the horny young bucks thinking what a fine fucking machine they had all for themselves. It also might be something they cherished enough for them to invest some time in finding her and restoring her to their camp.

"You figure they followed you?" he asked.

She swallowed hard. "I had hoped maybe they'd gave up."

"What do you think?" he asked Paco.

He looked up with his good eye and made a stern face. "No way. I figure they'll be along."

"We better post a guard."

"If we don't want some skinning knife at our throat, we better. I'll take the first watch."

Somewhere out in the twilight, a coyote yodeled at the moon and another answered. The quarter moon was about to rise. Slocum nodded in agreement. "Guess we better keep ourselves well armed and ready for them."

"That's the way I see it."

"They ever say what tribe they belonged to?" Slocum asked her.

She looked up from her cooking and shook her head. "They only spoke some bad Spanish. Mostly swear words and I never understood much else. They were Comanches, I know that."

Rising to pour them more coffee, she shook her head as if caught in deep thought. "I tried to hide my tracks for a day."

"Don't matter. They can find signs where white men would give up."

"You worry me." With the pot in her hand, as Slocum watched, she faced the night wind, and it softly shifted her hair and began to cool the temperature.

"We'll all have to become aware." Slocum blew on his steaming coffee to cool it.

"Señora, those bucks won't get you again. They will only lose their lives in this camp," Paco said.

She nodded that she'd heard him and set the pot down at the fire's edge. "They are cunning and cruel killers."

Slocum agreed.

The meal of rice and beef was as good as he could recall. When he looked to Paco for his opinion, he agreed. "Señora, she is good—no, it is very good food."

With a head shake to dismiss their praise, she looked embarrassed by their words. "I just fixed what you had. There will be enough, I think, for the morning."

"Plenty," Slocum said, and cradled his cup in his palm.

"I am going to slip out of camp and set up a guard," Paco said.

Slocum agreed with: "Wake me."

"I will, amigo." With a rifle in his right hand, Paco slipped off into the night.

"He is a good man," she said.

Slocum agreed and finished his coffee. "We better turn in."

"May I sleep with you?"

He considered her request and his bathless condition. "I'm grubby, dirty—ah—"

"No, I want to sleep in your arms. I'm sorry if I am so forward. But I feel it's the only way I'll sleep."

He nodded that he understood, and when she finished washing the few dishes and utensils, he picked up his bedroll. "I don't ever sleep close to the fire. First place invaders look."

She softly agreed, and followed him into the starlight to a place where he scuffed away with the side of his boot the sticks and clods from his intended bed site. Bedroll unfurled, he sat and removed his boots and socks. When he glanced up, she was dutifully unbuttoning the shirt. He undid his and hung it on a bush, then his pants. Seated on his butt, he felt her bare arm slip around his neck and a bare breast brush his arm as she settled in his lap.

"Hold me."

His arms engulfed her and he tucked her to his chest. Feeling the emerging erection beginning to be born under her, he looked into her eyes and all his guilt about his whiskers and no bath was swept away. Their mouths sought each other with a hungriness that bordered on madness. Her arms around his neck, her nipples were buried in his skin like steel roses on stems. Her palms clutched his bristled cheeks as she sought more and more. In his mouth, her hot tongue flamed with her needs.

Then she reached between them and began to glide her hand up and down his hardened tool. At last breathless, she shoved him down on his back with the flat of her hand and scurried furiously to rise up, then settled with a sharp cry when her tight ring passed his hammerhead. Like a jumping jack, she bounced on him. Her walls began to contract and his blood-swollen dick felt on fire when she slipped off him with a soft: "Please, get on top."

He moved between her white legs, which spread apart, and was grateful to be back buried in her hot cunt. As he drove it into her, she arched her back to receive all of him. They both strove to reach the next plateau of pleasure in a hard-fought battle. Then lightning struck his butt and an unseen hand crushed his gonads and he exploded inside her.

Exhausted, they collapsed in a pile. Her form curved with her back against his stomach, and his arm wrapped over her, one hand softly cradling her breast. Beneath the thin flannel blanket he had spread over both of them, he savored the warmth and the smoothness of her skin. What a way to go to sleep.

5

"Wake up," Paco whispered. "Both of you. We got company."

"How many?" Slocum threw the blanket back and reached for his shirt.

Paco squatted a few feet from them in the starlight; the rifle over his lap made a dull glint in the starlight. "Maybe all of them."

"Where are they?" Keeping low, Slocum sat and struggled to pull on his pants knowing he didn't need to be a silhouette against the sky. Britches on, he lay back and buttoned them.

"When you get that white shirt on, put a blanket over it or you'll make a target," he said to Mary.

He knew she was trembling in fear. To comfort her, he reached over and clutched her arms under the blanket she used for cover. "We won't let them get you."

Woodenly, she nodded and acknowledged she'd heard him. He handed her the shirt, and she scrambled to put it on while he pulled on his socks. "They on foot?" he asked Paco.

"I think they left their horses back in a wash west of here. That's how I heard them. Their horses coughed and Roan gave them his gruff whinny."

"He's pissed 'cause he's had my saddle on him all night anyway. Mary, follow me. Paco, you go south and we'll go north and try to circle around them."

38

"I guess we better shoot them." Paco said with a wary shake of his head.

"We better. It's us or them."

Dressed, Mary squatted beside Slocum, hugging her arms as if cold. "I'm afraid."

He reached over and squeezed her shoulder. "We can handle them."

"They're very tough."

"Ah, Señora, we won't let them have you."

She nodded at the man, but Slocum saw the fear in her eyes and realized how scared she had become since they awoke. He looked across the silver-lighted brush—somewhere out there was a silent enemy. Be a lot better if she wasn't here. Then he and Paco could use stealth against them.

"Which way you think they will come in here?"

"They may split—" Paco shrugged. "They may come as four. Boys aren't always smart."

Slocum agreed. Herding her low, they headed north. The six-gun was in his fist—his eyes straining in the night for any sign lost in shadows. Paco covered their backs with the rifle.

"When I say get flat, you get on your belly," he whispered to her.

She nodded and they moved catlike through the mesquite. Then, when they reached a dry wash, he indicated for her to get in it. No sign of the enemy. Soon they were moving westward down the wash—his plan was to cut them off from their own horses.

He saw an outline and stopped her. A buck was sitting up on a high point. Obviously the horse guard, though he had not seen the intruders sneaking up on him.

Paco indicated the seated Indian with the rifle in his hand. Slocum nodded. They needed to take him. It would put the others on alert, but that would reduce the count.

"We also need to gather their horses," he said in Mary's ear.

The rifle shot shattered the night. The buck half-rose and fell over, hit hard. Paco ran for his vantage point while Slocum and Mary raced to find the mounts. The horses were spooked by the shot, but not too bad. Slocum cut the rawhide hobbles as she gathered their jaw-bridle reins.

"Bring them," he said to her, and barreled up the slope to join his partner. On the ground beside Paco, he listened to his own hard breathing and for any telltale sounds. Nothing.

"I'm going to our horses. They'll head there next if they aren't at them already. Keep her here."

Paco nodded. "Be careful, *mi amigo.*"

"Always—" He took off running low to the left. Five shots in his Army model Colt .44, if he hadn't lost a cap off one of the nipples and didn't have a misfire. But the gun had been dry. A bareheaded figure rose and drew back a bow. Slocum took a snap shot and dove to the right. Belly-down on the gravely soil, he dared not stick his head up too high. The Colt armed and ready, he listened to hear if he'd hit his target or not.

Then he heard the soft pad of someone running toward him. Obviously leaping over brush and running pell-mell in his direction, no doubt coming to the aid of the bow shooter. Slocum gathered up and rose, pistol ready and cocked.

The handgun spoke a red-orange flame at the dark figure not forty feet away. The attacker threw a lance that whizzed by Slocum. His second shot staggered the Comanche. The bullet cut off the war cry in his throat. Heart thumping, Slocum surveyed the pearl-lighted brush. Where was number four?

Then he heard Roan grunt, and knew in a second the young buck had mistaken the horse for one broken to ride because he was under a saddle. In the night's dim light, he watched the youth pile in the saddle and Roan fly into the sky on springs. It was a ride Slocum would not miss taking. The rider looked like a sack of chaff being whipped all over the seat, desperately pulling leather, and in the end was pitched high and far.

Slocum hurried to find him. With his .44 ready, he found the crumpled near-naked body with his head strangely twisted aside—he'd broken his neck in the fall.

"Whew, that roan can buck. Any more?" Paco asked, joining him.

Slocum searched around and, satisfied, saw Mary leading four Indian ponies. "No, he's the last. The others may not be dead."

Paco nodded. "Take her to camp. They will be."

Slocum agreed, holstered his six-gun, and went to help her.

"Are they—" Her eyes were asking him for the truth.

"All dead."

She closed her lids and dropped her chin. He threw his arm over her and hugged her. "It's over."

"No," she sobbed. "It will never be over for me."

"Yes, it will. Pain goes away. The memory will be buried behind the good things that happen later."

He let go of the horses' leads. They would not go far anyway, and he held her in his arms. She deserved to cry and get it out of her system. Maybe she could go back home and be a housewife—a mother again. But he knew too that society often treated captives as little more than *soiled merchandise.* But perhaps she could shed that image too—Mary was strong.

6

Paco chose a moon lake for their camp. There were lots of well-broken steers and cows that spooked some at their approach, but running yoked in pairs was not highly successful. Paco roped one of them by the heels. Slocum ran in and unyoked the free one first. The wooden stocks were removed from number two, and the rope released with a flip or two. When freed, some ran off and bucked like a horse with a cougar on its back. Others strolled off matching their mate's stride like they were still yoked.

Late in the afternoon, they released a pair of four-year-old steers. The two instantly took adversary positions, and Slocum kept his eye on them, quickly remounting Ute. Bellowing with anger, they charged one another and began a ground-churning struggle. Horns clashed and blood flew off the sharp tips. Again and again they rammed each other, neither giving an inch. Between rams, a red flood from one of the combatants' nostrils was flung along with a stream of snot shaken off its shoulders. The show looked to be a fight that could only end in the death of one of the close-matched opponents.

Paco slapped his leg and laughed at their ferocious battle. "Whew, they worked up a real mad being hitched together. We can come back for that yoke."

"I ain't getting between those two hornets. They don't

know they're steers yet either," Slocum said, and turned Ute for camp.

"Pretty damn dumb. Hey, *toro,* you have no *huevos.* Save your energy." Paco's laughter rang out as they rode back to camp.

"I'll have to say the yoking works. They're a lot more settled than they would have been simply turned loose after working them."

"Ah; *sí,* the colonel knew what he was doing. It was an expensive plan, but there was no other way," Paco agreed.

"If those cattle bring anything at all and he can get them to Missouri, he may be a rich man."

They trotted for their camp and some of Mary's cooking. Dead tired from all the roping on day five, Slocum wondered why the colonel hadn't come to join them like he'd said. The piles of yokes beside the wagon tracks grew taller. Some cattle they caught only wore broken half-yokes; with others, one member had escaped and the animal left behind had a twisted neck from dragging the yoke to water and graze.

When their tails were bobbed so they could be recognized as the worked ones, Slocum saw many others had joined them that weren't branded and marked. Cattle being communal animals, they'd joined the tamer ones. Still, the unworked acted more wary, even if they weren't headed for the brush at the first sight of Slocum and Paco on horseback.

Wearing a blanket skirt and old straw hat and Slocum's shirt, Mary looked fresh. Bathing in the small lake at night, they were all a shade cleaner and more refreshed. But a day's work erased most of the previous night's efforts to clean up. No matter, Slocum was pleased to see her looking so uplifted.

Hands on her hips, she looked up from her cooking and laughed at them when they rode in. "What's the tally today?"

"We've de-yoked a hundred head." Slocum dropped heavily from the saddle and rested while his sea legs found circulation.

"What did he pay for the yokes?" she asked, using her hand against the glare.

"Some twenty-five *centavos*." Paco slapped his stirrup up on the saddle and jerked loose the sweat-soaked latigos. "There are many poor people on the border. They brought them up here by ox *carretas* that were stacked very high. See, there is no screw and ring in them to hook a pull chain. That saved him much money. They are carved from cottonwood and are kind of crude. The neck piece is willow."

"Willow grows along the Rio Grande?"

Paco nodded. "Oh, the yokes made lots of work for some poor peons."

"Yes, and they had nothing else to do," said Slocum. "He paid us a dollar to rope them. Twelve cents a head for a yoke. Mustangs for the taking. The food bill for his hands and new rope. He'll head for Missouri with eight hundred to a thousand head next spring. May restore him to his old status in life." Slocum swept his saddle off and a hot breath escaped the saddle and pads. He stood the saddle on the horn for the wool lining to dry.

"You know, amigo, some men need to be rich."

Slocum nodded and took the hot coffee Mary offered in a tin cup. "To each his own, compadre."

"Ah, Señora, you spoil me." Paco took his cup and nodded at her in appreciation. "I will never again be able to eat the bad food Lopez serves."

"And where will you go when the cattle-catching is over?" she asked.

"Ah, to Mexico. To see my little ones and my wife Camille."

"What are they doing without you?"

"Tending a few hectares that have water to raise many good things like corn and beans and melons and peppers. Some fine fruit trees. Raising me some fine colts to race and waiting for their papa to come home, I guess." He dropped to the ground and his spur rowels rang. Seated cross-legged, he swept off his wide sombrero and combed back his dark hair that curled around the edges.

"When will the colonel get here?" she asked.

"I looked for him yesterday," Paco said, and looked at Slocum for his thoughts.

"Even in an oxcart he should be here by now."

"Perhaps we should go see about him *mañana*."

"You want to go?" Slocum asked her.

"Yes—I want to be with you two." She brought them both plates heaped with beef and beans.

"That's the last of the calf we butchered," she said, handing Paco his supper.

"We'll get another after we find the colonel," Slocum said, watching her take a plate for herself. Grateful that her appetite was back, he busied himself eating.

"I may ride ole Roan," he said between bites.

"Oh, well, we want to see that." Paco winked his good eye at her.

"Be the day to break him in. Snub him up to your big dun, Paco, and we can get half the edge off him in a few miles."

Paco nodded as if he hadn't thought of such a thing. "Time we get to the colonel, he may be a new kitten, huh, Señora?"

"We'll see."

Slocum and Paco took turns guarding at night. Neither man was satisfied that more Comanche might not come to avenge the dead ones if they found out what happened to them. So after midnight, Slocum left Mary in the blankets and went to a high point with the Spencer repeater across his lap in the evaporating heat. The night wind's soft whispers in his ear, he studied the horses for anything that made them curious. Mostly, they grunted in sleep. Still, this was a land where one could in a heartbeat trade his life for death.

Far away, a coyote howled in yapping fashion, another answered, and they were gone on some nocturnal hunt for small deer or rabbit. Not the deep howl of buffalo wolf he'd heard on the plains of Kansas—ole coyote was a lesser predator and stayed back until his larger cousin was ready for him to have the carrion left. Even then, in times of poor hunting, the coyote became a meal for the wolf.

Before the sun came up, Mary joined him, taking a seat on the ground beside him. Her voice smoky with sleep and soft in the silence now that the night insects were at last asleep, she said, "Be careful with Roan today. He's a stout one."

He looked off at the eastern rim for the first tint of light. "That's why I want him broke."

"I know it is the little boy coming out. You want to be number one."

"No, he's mine and I want him broke enough to carry me out of this thorny hot land someday."

"Where will you go?"

"They say the Bighorn Mountains are pretty."

"Where are they?"

"West and north of Fort Laramie."

"You ever been there?"

"No. But I haven't been many places."

She glanced over at him. "Why are you in Texas?"

"I thought Texas was recovering—" He dropped his gaze to the rifle in his lap. "It's as poor as the rest of the South."

"Will the South ever recover?"

He pulled some dry grass stems and scattered them in the soft wind. "Not in our lifetimes, I fear."

"Where can we go?"

He glanced over at her. Did she consider herself as his woman? We? Had he promised her anything?

"When this is over, I'll take you back to Fredricksburg."

With several nods, she said softly, "I understand."

He wasn't sure she did understand. Making roots was still not even possible for him. Had his ploy worked back in Fort Smith? Only time would tell if the federal authorities had closed the books on him. And all his big plans to go home after the smoke cleared from the war and pick up the pieces lay shattered behind him.

"I better make a fire." She started to get up. "Are we going to find the colonel today?"

"We'll try. That's the plan." He pulled her over and kissed her cheek, then let go.

She smiled at him and went off in the starlight to make

them breakfast. On the way, she toed Paco's form in his bedroll. "Time to get up, hombre."

"Ah," he said, sitting up and chuckling softly. "To be woke up by an angel's foot is so nice."

Her laughter peeled out. Busy building the fire on her knees, she shook her head in amusement at his words. "My, my, you do make a girl feel good."

"Oh, you need encouragement in such a place as this. You seen anything?" Paco asked Slocum when he ambled into their camp.

"Nothing. The horses are acting calm. We've made it through another night unscathed."

Paco ran his fingers through his hair as if examining it. "I really like my scalp."

"So would they." Slocum grinned and stretched his arms over his head. The sun would be up in a few minutes and start percolating the day's temperature.

"We better find the colonel or what's left of him," Paco said, rolling up his bedding and binding it tight with rawhide strings.

"It's damn funny he isn't up here with the crew," Slocum said, perplexed by the situation.

"Something is wrong," Paco said, and Slocum agreed.

With that possible turn of events on his mind, Slocum went and caught Roan to ride. It would be a hard day, but he wanted the stout horse ready. Somewhere in the recesses of his mind there was a need and place for the horse in the days ahead. If nothing more, it would be a better way to leave than the way he'd come to this land—aboard Judas, the donkey.

Horses packed, the men seated on the ground, they ate Mary's breakfast of leftover beef and brown rice with hot coffee. She fire-baked some bread, and both men nodded in approval at the meal when she delivered the hot biscuits.

"Better eat," Slocum said to her.

"I will. I figure we won't eat again till dark, so fill up."

"Ah, you spoil us, Señora. Spoil us bad."

She laughed and took up her own plate.

After the dishes were washed and stored, they tied down

the last pack and she rode Ute to lead the packhorses. Paco
snubbed the upset Roan to his saddle horn, and Slocum
eased over to his horse to slip into the saddle. When his
weight was on Roan's back, he tried to break loose and
pitch, but there was no way the horse could get enough slack
to do more than shake his head. Rollers went out his flared
nostrils in protest. His screams and grunts rolled across the
greasewood. But all he could do was try to back away and
shake his head in frustrated fury.

For his stubbornness, he was flailed on the butt with
Slocum's braided rope reins. Slocum could also jerk on the
bosal and punish him. In a short while Roan matched Paco's
dun's trot—not willingly, but forced to obey or be dragged.
In mid-morning, Paco handed Slocum the lead and they rode
on. Roan began to engage in some head-tossing as if to test
his confinement, and then, as if satisfied to be free, kept up
the pace with the others. His shoulder dark with the sweat
drawn out by his own nervousness, he breathed free and not
hard. No telling how tough he really could be. When Slocum
turned and winked at Mary, she nodded in approval, bringing on the pack animals.

At noontime, they took a break at a small mud hole and
watered the horses. That gave her a chance to slip off into
the brush and relieve herself. Slocum drank some hot canteen water—better than the shallow stuff the horses sucked
up where they could find enough to do it. Many got on one
knee to drink from the meager supply. Desert-raised animals know more tricks than those brought up in towns.
Slocum caught the leads and helped Mary into the saddle.
Then he turned and looked at the hip-shot Roan. He'd see
about him.

Cheeking the bosal headstall up to his left leg to contain
the big horse, he mounted and Roan circled impatiently underneath him. Fretting, Roan danced on eggs the first hundred yards, with Slocum ready to saw his nose off. The bosal
could shut his air off if pulled hard enough. Paco shouted
something, but Roan was headed south in a long trot and
Slocum smiled to himself.

It was the dark streak in the sky that began to concern Slocum by mid-afternoon. A black trace of smoke from a hot fire marked the sky, not some campfire, but the sort that came from lots of things burning. Slocum tossed his head in that direction.

"I see it too," Paco said with a grim look pasted on his swarthy face.

"What is it?" Mary asked in a small voice, searching their faces as she booted Ute in closer.

"No telling," Slocum said. "One of us ought to ride ahead and see what we can learn."

Paco nodded. "I can go see."

"Be careful. Sometimes they lay traps like that to get the curious."

Paco indicated he'd heard him and set spurs to the dun.

"I'm worried," she said, looking around at the gray sea of greasewood and dead brush.

"We'll take care of you."

"I know, but there could be many of them."

"We'll be fine."

"I hope so. . . ."

Paco soon disappeared in the heat wayes. Slocum could regret deciding to break the big horse before that day was over—it was not nearly as dependable as one of his string. Not even broken to rein worth much. Slocum had to plow-rein him around in a wide circle to get close enough to talk to Mary. It would be good to know the cause of the fire and the source.

"What—what should we do?" she asked.

"Keep moving that way. More than likely we're too late to help them."

"Too late. You think they're dead?"

"Easy, easy, girl. Whatever was set on fire is burned by now is what I mean."

Her emphatic head shake and look showed him the fear and disappointment she felt. Maybe it would all turn out to be an innocent thing. But the rock in the pit of his stomach told him that whatever lay ahead was serious.

He reined up at the sight of Paco coming back on the run. "What happened?"

The grim look on his face answered half his question. "Boys are dead. Shot in their sleep—" He checked his hard-breathing horse dancing under him.

"No one alive?"

"I didn't see Lopez or the colonel."

"We better go bury them."

Paco nodded.

"Who did it?" she asked.

"I ain't sure it was Comanch—them boys was shot in the face at close range."

Slocum frowned. Who else could have done it? He motioned for Paco to lead the way and then looked at Mary. "Whoever did it—we'll find 'em."

She agreed with a grim look and jerked on her pack string to make them come on. In a half hour, they'd know more.

7

Writing in his own blood with a finger for a pen, Lopez had scrawled MATT on a flour sack. Slocum held it in his hands and read it standing in the smoke of the smoldering yokes and wagon. They'd found the cook's body on the far side of camp.

"I never figured he could write," Paco said, squatted down beside Slocum, looking over his shoulder at the man's scrawl.

"He passed first grade with this note." Slocum shook it in his hands, filled with bitterness and rage. "Matt was mad at him for running him off. Came back and got his revenge. Man, he cut him up and left him to die a sorry death."

He averted his look from Lopez's bloody body and the flies feeding on the black blood. The sight was more than upsetting—worse than the powder-burn-speckled faces of the crew members with round dark holes drilled in their un-sunbaked foreheads where hats had kept the skin shaded—two in the kid's face inches apart. Slocum had closed the boy's wide fear-filled eyes. Matt had aimed to be damn sure he was dead.

"Wanted it to look like Indios did it," Paco said.

"Yeah, give them the blame. No sign of the colonel's body?" Slocum asked him.

"None." Paco shook his head as if confused by not finding any sign of him. "I circled all around. He never crawled off where I can see."

"There's a shovel that escaped the fire." Slocum pushed off his knees to straighten up. "We better bury them."

"*Sí.* Maybe they know in Rio Frio where Matt is at?"

"We can go see about him after the burying. Matt must've stolen the horses. No sign of them, is there?"

"They were drove away from the tracks I've seen."

"Broke horses would sell easier than range cattle. The colonel had a few good ones. I liked the big gray he rode. He ever mention to you about having a wife or family?"

Paco blinked his good eye and shook his head as if in deep consideration. "No."

With a blanket Mary brought him, Slocum covered the old man's body. "Comanche ain't the only ones that get brutal."

She acknowledged his words, looking pale and shaken by the turn of events. "I thought . . . only Indians did such things."

"The world's full of savages in all colors."

"This was a real lesson in that. What do you think happened to the colonel?"

"No telling, but the sight of this tells me it probably was not good." Not good at all. "We better get them buried and ride into Rio Frio."

The sun dying in the west cast the last long shadows of the day across the hot breathless land. Slocum sat cross-legged on the ground and reviewed the incident. The scene of carnage and the subsequent mass burial had filled him with many ill feelings. Matt had turned into a mad-dog killer. Those three cowboys had done nothing to him to deserve to be executed. The whole thing was the insane act of a rabid individual.

Obviously, Matt must have recruited some others like ghouls to assist him in the slaughter of the outfit. Slocum would cross their path again and even the score for the outfit. He looked up as Paco dropped to squat on his boot heels close by him.

"*Mi amigo,* what should we do?"

"Go to the village and see if we can learn anything about the colonel."

"What if we learn nothing?"

Slocum looked off in the dimming twilight. "I count between five and seven hundred head of cattle we could drive to Sedalia. If we could find some horses and cowboys, we could drive them up there."

"I could find some vaqueros across the border. But how would we feed them?"

"On credit. With a herd of cattle we could get some credit."

Paco shook his head. "I don't savvy . . . cred-it."

"It's when they advance you money on the strength of your assets."

"Oh, that is even worse." He clapped Slocum on the shoulder. "I leave that to you. You think the colonel is dead?"

Slocum nodded slowly. "Or he would be here."

"Maybe so. But what if he is alive?"

"Then we'll get the cattle together for him."

Paco shifted his weight to his other leg. "You ever been to Missouri?"

"No, but I'd never been to Texas before and I found you."

With a wide grin, Paco shook his head and pushed his sombrero back on his shoulders. "What will we do for horses?"

"Catch them. They're for free and all it takes is hard work."

"Whew!" He sliced the sweat off his forehead with his trigger finger. "Break wild horses. Borrow money. Find vaqueros. Go to Missouri. How far is it away?"

"A couple of months."

"A couple of months? It must be a long ways."

Slocum agreed as Mary's fire glow began to reflect from their faces. "But what else have we got to do?"

"Nothing. I ride with you, *mi amigo.*"

"Good," Slocum said, and hoped the man never regretted it.

"We're going to town in the morning," he said to Mary when she brought him a plate of steaming frijoles.

She paused and then nodded, straightening her back as if stiff. "I'll bring yours in a minute," she said to Paco. "Then tonight I want to go down to the lake and bathe."

"I'll go along," said Slocum.

"I'll be fine."

"I'll still go—you can't tell about Comanches."

"Fine." With a swish of her blanket skirt, she went for Paco's plate; after that, she joined them amid the sound of the creaking insects. Somewhere, a coyote cut the night with his yipping, then a chorus joined him.

After they ate, she washed the tinware and came with a flour-sack towel to where he sat smoking a roll-your-own from Paco.

"I'm ready."

"Fine," he said, and rose to his feet. He could feel the stiffness from the grave-digging in his arms and shoulders. "We'll be back, Paco."

"*Sí*. Have a good time getting wet." His laughter shattered the starlit world. "Should we be on guard?"

"Get some sleep. I'll watch things for a while."

"I can do that. Wake me later. Thanks, Señora, for the meal."

"You're welcome." They were off through the knee-high greasewood headed for the lake.

Slocum fell in behind her on the path. Over his shoulder, a quarter moon began to rise. He'd be grateful for the light.

"This cattle business isn't getting you home," he said.

She turned and shook her head to dismiss his concern. "I am so glad to be free, I don't really care."

"It may be months before we are even close to your home."

"Don't worry about me—I am at ease in your camp."

He nodded that he understood. Perhaps there was less at home for her, knowing that her husband and son were dead.

That alone would be tough enough for her to go back and face, besides wondering how folks would react to learning of the repeated rapes by her captors.

At the edge of the shiny water, she began to undress. He found a place to scrape aside the rocks and sticks and sit on the ground. Since she didn't seem to mind him viewing her, he took in her movements in the silver light. Clear of the blouse and skirt, she went gingerly over the deep pocks of dried cow tracks to the edge. Then, like an otter, she waded in and began to swim. Her wet shoulders glowed as her arms reached out for each stroke. At last, she stood on the far side and wiped her face with her hands.

"Come on. Join me." She waved to him.

"It could be dangerous."

"Come on. I'm not afraid."

"Maybe you should be."

"All I worry about is being accepted at home."

He nodded and rose to toe off his boots. "I understand."

Then, standing on one foot at a time, he shed his socks. Next came his shirt, and he slid off his pants exposing his skin to the still-hot night air. His clothes hung over a bush, he set out like a sore-toed bear over the stiff obstacles. Damn, how did she go about so easy barefoot all the time? He'd have to find her some footwear in town.

Sandy mud oozed between his toes as he waded toward her in the warm water. She never moved. She stood there as if waiting for him. When he drew close, she put out her arms and he swept her into his own. Her firm, teardrop breasts pressed into his lower chest and he savored their closeness.

He bent over and kissed her. Their lips locked and their hungry tongues sought each other. They were alone on another planet, aeons away from the memory of brutal murders and all the troubles that plagued them.

When at last they separated, out of breath, she softly laughed at him. "You forgot to bring a blanket."

"I did," he said, hugging her tight in his arms. "What shall I do?"

"Dry off and go find one," she said in a small voice.

They slipped into camp and carried his bedroll away from the snoring Paco to a place apart where Slocum scraped the trash and sticks clear with the side of his boot. She unfurled the bedroll and made certain it was devoid of any lumps under the ground cloth. While she did that, he toed off his boots and shucked his clothing.

Realizing he was undressed, she sat up on her knees and undid the shirt's buttons. "I have waited for this time."

"I have waited until you were sure." He dropped down in front of her and took her in his arms as she fought loose the strings at her waist. She rose and shed the skirt, then hurried back to face him.

"I am never sure of—of anything in my life since that day." She sniffed and then buried her face on his shoulder. "But I have tried to forget—oh, don't worry if I cry. I need to cry a lot—not about you and me—I mean here, tonight. . . ."

"It's all right." He squeezed her tight. She felt good in his arms. He knew many fears had consumed her since he'd found her—maybe from here on she could recover and find her place in life.

"Love me and have me. Oh, I am so wanton, God forgive me."

He covered her mouth with his. Her breasts hard against him, he sought the fire of her tongue. Set afire, they both could not get enough oral attention. Then he spilled her on the bedroll and tasted her left nipple. Traces of the water's gyp taste filled his mouth as he devoured her breasts and she squirmed in pleasure. Soft moans escaped her lips as she clutched his head to her.

His tongue traced a downward path on her body, and she gasped in recognition of his purpose. Her fingers combed anxiously through his hair, clutching and releasing him to flatten and then hunch her shoulders in wild expectation of his lips on her skin.

A sharp cry escaped her lips when he gathered her legs

up and began to kiss her gates. Unable to stand it a moment longer, she pulled him upward. "Now. Now."

Her body trembled in anticipation of his entry. He moved forward over her, heady drunk on wanting to take her. Underneath him, he eased his erection into her wet gates and she spread her legs wider. Her strong hands clutched him when the swollen head passed her tight ring. With her bare heels beating a tattoo on the back of his calves, he felt the waves of her contractions with each plunge into her nest. Harder and harder, his buttocks ached to be completely inside her. Again and again he sought the depth of her, until she hunched up and gave a short groan—she'd come.

For a second she went limp; then, shaking free of the delirium, she reached up and cupped his face in her hands to kiss him on the mouth.

"Go," she whispered, and settled back. In minutes she was wild again, head tossing her hair in her face. Raising her butt off the blankets to meet his charge, she hunched hard at him in total abandonment. Her fingernails raked his back and she even bit him on the chest—then he drove deep and the tickling in his scrotum began. With a hard effort, he drove himself against her pubic bone, grinding their coarse hair between them and exploding inside her.

She fainted under him. Braced over her, he could do nothing but smile down on her in the starlight. "You all right?"

"I think so."

"Think so?"

She pulled him down on top of her. "How would I know? How can I feel so—so fulfilled and still want more?"

"Your womanhood has blossomed."

"What does that mean?"

"You found out you're a woman."

"But I was married—had a nice husband—even had a son." She shook her head in dismay. "And here I am. Wanting more of you and what you have done to me tonight."

"We have to savor life as we go—it's a short time here."

"Trust me. I won't waste any ever again." She reached underneath him and squeezed his half-hard dick in her fingers. "Let's not talk about it—now."

"Fine," he said, scooting his blanket-burned knees forward to follow her reinsertion.

"Send me away again," she said, and threw her arms out in abandonment for him to take her.

And he did.

8

A low profile of jacales sat on the flat land. Rio Frio huddled on the dusty plains bathed in heat waves under the mid-morning sun.

"What if the killers are there?" Paco motioned with a head toss toward the village.

"I guess we can deal with them."

"You have no bad feelings about this—no worries that they might be waiting for us?" Paco shrugged under his vest.

"There is no one to buy his stolen horses there."

"Ah, you make a good notion, *mi amigo*. No horse buyers in Rio Frio. Why did I not think of that?"

"You aren't a money man."

Paco slapped his great saddle horn with his palm. "You are my banker. Huh, Señora, he is our banker?"

"We're leaving all that to Slocum." She smiled at the Mexican.

"Good. You have any money?" Slocum asked him.

"A few pesos, why?"

"I have some too. We need to pool our money here and now."

She threw her hands up, riding between the two. "I have none."

"Here is mine," Paco said, and tossed him the leather purse. "There is not much there."

Slocum nodded that he understood. "Let's trot. We have much to do in this place."

"What about the colonel?" Paco asked, holding up his horse before they took off.

"If he's not in the village, I'm not sure what happened to him."

"Nor me. Let's ride."

Slocum met the man who owned the dusty store, Herman Goeserman. A man with dark hard eyes and stiff black hair, Goeserman spoke with a German accent whether in Spanish or English.

"No, the colonel, he owes me no money. He was a very good customer. Paid cash. Vere is he?"

"We don't know. Some killers murdered the rest of the crew while we were up north unyoking cattle. We never found his body."

"Vot they do with it?"

"I ain't certain, but if he was alive, I figured he'd've shown up by now."

Grim-faced, Goeserman nodded. *"Ja."*

"Paco and I want to take those cattle to Missouri. But we'd need some supplies to ever get there."

"How much?"

"Enough frijoles, rice, lard, baking powder, flour, corn-meal, raisons, sugar, and coffee for a crew."

Goeserman squeezed his pointed beard and nodded as if in deep thought over the matter. "Maybe several hundred pesos, huh?"

"Yes, sir."

"But you own no land around here. Why would you come back and pay me?"

" 'Cause I always pay my debts."

The German shook his head. "But I don't know you. What if you fall off your horse and drown going there?"

"Then Paco or Mary will bring you your money." Slocum glanced at them and they both nodded.

With a suspicious cut of his black eyes, Goeserman nodded slowly. "I expect to double my money for such a risk."

"Fair enough."

"So what now?"

Slocum hooked a thumb at Mary. "She needs a riding skirt and a few blouses, a hairbrush, a new straw hat, and some footwear."

The storekeeper made a "hmmm" sound from his nose and nodded. Then he called out, "Gresalda."

A short Mexican woman appeared, and he talked in Spanish to her about Mary's needs.

The smiling woman bowed and then invited Mary into the back. She waved her inside holding the blanket doorway.

"They burned his wagon," Slocum said. "We'll need to find one."

"There is high-iron-wheel *carreta* someone abandoned." Goeserman indicated the rear of the store. "You can take it."

"Paco, go look at it."

The man nodded and with a ring of his silver spur rowels, hurried out the front door to do Slocum's bidding. Satisfied, Slocum turned back to the storekeeper. "Good man."

"He moves well for a Mexican."

"He is going to Mexico and find some vaqueros tomorrow. We won't waste any time getting going—horses to break, and we'll round them up and head north."

"You can never make it before winter."

"Banks had a place at Mason, he said, where he was going to winter them."

"He paid me cash. I know nothing of a place up there."

"He ever mail a letter from here?"

Goeserman shrugged. "No, but he got one once."

"You see who wrote him?"

"A lawyer in San Antonio."

"What was his name?"

Goeserman shook his head. "I can't remember. But it was a lawyer."

"That's a lead anyway."

"Ah, dere are many of them dere."

"I agree. Will he pay me if he is alive?"

"Yes."

"Good. Now I got to go to work."

Slocum turned when he heard Paco coming back. "How's the rig?"

"Great. Why did they abandon it?" Paco asked.

"They took pack mules into Mexico instead," said Goeserman.

"Well, won't they come back for it?"

Goeserman shook his head to dismiss any concern. "Banditos killed them in Mexico and took their mules and all their supplies."

"Tough country," Slocum said. "Murderers, cutthroats, and Comanches."

"Comanches?" Goeserman's face paled under his white complexion.

"They held her captive," Slocum said in a low voice. "Killed her husband and son."

Goeserman pointed to the side door with a frown. "That woman in there?"

"Yes. Why?"

"She is lucky to even be alive."

Slocum shook his head. "Maybe, maybe not."

"What do you mean?"

"Folks don't always accept the women who come back. You understand?"

Goeserman nodded. "Yes, that is very sad."

"Paco and I will look after her and find her a place where she will be accepted."

"You are a strange man. May be why I trust you will try to repay me."

"I'll do my damnedest. May I look in on the sewing party?"

"Sure, go ahead."

He stuck his head in the door and saw Mary and four women busy cutting and sewing on material. She smiled excitedly and stood up. "They are sewing me three outfits. Two for riding, one for regular life."

"Stay there. Paco and I are going for a drink. We'll be back later. We have a wagon. Not a big one, but a wagon."

"Good. I'm excited. Can you two afford three outfits?"

He told her it was no problem and winked at her. "We'll be anxious to see you wear them."

"No more blanket skirt." She laughed, and the joy rang out. Even the other women seemed excited for her, jabbering in Spanish.

Dialgo looked up and blinked when they entered the cantina. "Ah, the cowboys are here."

"No, just us two. You seen the one called himself Matt lately?"

The barkeep shook his head. "Not in weeks."

"Well, him and some renegades killed the rest of the crew. We can't find the colonel either and they stole the outfit's horses."

"Mother of God. Why did they do that for?"

"'Cause they're mean sonsabitches."

"I mean, mean—oh, they killed that horny boy?" Dialgo arched his eyebrows in shock.

"Shot him in the forehead. Then made sure he was dead."

"Who was with him—with this Matt?"

Slocum rested his forearms on the bar. "Damned if we know."

"Took all the horses?" Dialgo paused before filling the two shot glasses he set on the bar.

"Yes."

"What will they do with them?"

"Sell 'em for money. Only things worth a damn out there," Paco said.

Dialgo looked from one to the other. "The colonel—what did they do to him?"

"Damned if we know," Slocum said, and held up the glass to look at the clarity of the whiskey. "We looked high and low for him."

"He was a great man."

Paco raised his glass. "To the colonel."

Slocum matched him. "To the colonel."

They both downed their drinks. Paco set his empty jigger on the bar. "One more, amigo, and then I will ride to Mexico and find us some vaqueros. What will we call this outfit?"

"Estrella Cattle Company," Slocum said

"Good name. We shoot for the stars, huh?"

Slocum counted him out a few dollars in case he couldn't bum a meal or needed a drink on the way. He shoved it over to him. "Be careful. No telling, we may be on Matt's death list too."

"I savvy that, amigo. You and her don't let your guard down either. The Comanche, he is out there, and this madman may come back too."

Slocum acknowledged he'd heard him. "How long will you be?' "

"Oh, maybe as long as a week. I wish to see my wife and the little ones."

"See them. We'll round up some more horses while you're gone and be ready for you."

"Ah, that will be much work."

"Maybe when we are old, we can sit back and say once we were crazy and went to Sedalia with a herd."

"I always wanted to see that place." Paco threw down the second shot with a gasp, then shook Slocum's hand and left for Mexico.

Slocum watched him push out the dusty batwing doors. He hoped his compadre had luck finding riders. If this halfbaked scheme of his was to work, they had to have them—like they had to have horses—lots of them. Fifty to sixty at least, plus two teams to pull the cart with the chuck items. It was a long way to Missouri, and he still didn't know if they could winter the herd at Mason. Good questions to ask. But no one was screaming answers at him.

Sundown came and he and Mary ate supper with the Goesermans. Herman's wife Gresalda was a pleasant Mexican woman who matched her husband's grumblings with cheery words. In another day, she promised, Mary's clothes would be completed. Mary wore the pleated skirt and blouse they'd made for her. In her new outfit, she looked radiant to Slocum.

"When will we go back?" Mary asked him privately at the table.

"When the clothes are finished. We need to round up some mustangs to break out for a string."

"Good, I get to help."

He cut her a sharp glance. "You may eat those words before it's over."

She made a face to dismiss his concern.

"Your hair looks nice."

"I finally can brush it. I have a brush."

They both laughed, and Goeserman frowned across the table at them. "Vat is so funny?"

"Mary finally has a hairbrush."

The German nodded like that was nothing and went back to eating. Slocum winked at her. Having a hairbrush of her own at last was a wonderful thing after living among savages without one for months. He tried to eat and forget the image of the horny bucks taking turns on her body. A wonder she still had her mind. But Mary was a survivor.

They left Rio Frio the next afternoon with enough food for them for a few weeks packed on two burros that Goeserman had found for them. They also had a spool of rope to make lariats, halters, leads, and tie-downs. Despite the old man's grumbling, he acted like he really was supporting their plans to make the drive—of course he'd earn plenty if they did. No doubt everything was charged to Slocum's account at double the cost of cash, but Slocum expected that to happen. Having the supplies would help insure their success.

They camped away from the burned-out wagon. He set up a shade made from tarp in some straggly wind-rustled cottonwoods that would be their protection. Mary wore a newer palm straw hat with a chin strap, moccasins, and a new riding outfit when they left camp to look for horses.

The first day, they scouted a large bunch led by a blood bay stallion. He was acting wary. Slocum moved west to try and turn them back toward the trap. The stud sent them northward—mares and colts, with some yearlings. Slocum really wanted some three-to-five-year-old studs and gelded ones that had never been caught since surgery. But that might be a big order. He and Mary stood in the stirrups, forcing their horses into a long trot on the west side of the herd with a dusty cloud coming from the mustangs.

"We need to turn them east," he said. "You bring them from the rear. I'm going to circle ahead and head them that way."

She nodded behind the bandanna mask that filtered out the dust.

He spurred his horse into a lope and began to gain ground on the herd. To avoid him, the mass swung east. The movement pleased him. With only two hands to round up horses, there were lots of problems. The roundup needed to be done at a distance, and then only to re-aim the herd where he wanted them to go. The billowing dust blinded him, and the herd's churning unshod feet added to it. The plaintive cries of colts separated from their mothers, the stallion's challenging screams, along with the drum of the herd's hooves, thundered across the land.

The sun swung westward. Slocum's lathered horse began to weaken under him and he wondered about Mary's. She rode far to his right behind them and obscured by the brown cloud. It had been an hour since he last saw her. He felt confident the mustangs were going at last in the general direction of the trap. Shouting at them, he beat his lariat on his leg to hurry their trip toward the catch pen.

He began to see the flying rags the colonel had strung on bushes to funnel them. The increase of the wind made the rags work better and the band shied from them. He dropped his jaded pony to a trot and pulled back to join Mary. At last, the horses were headed directly for the trap. The wind had lifted the dust. Obviously, they had used the water source inside before and weren't too spooked by the notion, for he could see them streaming toward it.

"We may have us a bunch caught," he shouted at her.

She pulled down the kerchief as they rode side by side. "Yes, and I'm excited."

He felt the same. If Paco could only find them the hands.

9

Sorting the horses was the task the next morning. Both on horseback, they cut mothers and colts out of the bunch. When the ones they wanted were cut from the others and in the last pen, they sent the rest out into the desert. They stopped and dismounted for a drink from their canteens. The water was tepid and had a chalky taste. Slocum wiped the back of his hand over his whiskered face.

"Well, girl, we've got about twenty horses in there that might make cow ponies."

"You intend to keep the stallion?" she asked.

"He'll make a stout one as a gelding."

She laughed at the proud horse pawing dirt and looking ready to fight them. "Well, old boy, you better get all you want. Your days are numbered."

Slocum swept her up and kissed her. "Don't worry about him. He's had his share, and a new young stud out there will fight to own his harem. Mother Nature picks the best."

"What now?"

"Take our horses back. They're done in." He rubbed his calloused palm on his whiskered face. "Maybe shave, bathe, and rest."

"Sounds great. How long will we be alone before Paco comes back?"

"Week or so. Why?"

She gave him a big knowing smile. "So if I want to drag you off to the blankets, I can as long as he isn't back."

"Any time, my lady." He gave her a playful shove and then mounted his horse. "Ain't no blanket up here."

"There is in camp."

He nodded, feeling good about the horses in the trap and ready for some celebrating with her.

A half hour later, they were back at the shade. The tarp was rippling overhead in the rising wind. His efforts to tighten the ropes soon drew down its tautness, so it made only a small flap in the rising breeze. That completed, he dropped on the ground and yawned. It was the reflection of light from a shiny item far off that made his hand shoot for his gun butt.

"Get down," he hissed. "There's someone out there."

She dropped down beside him. "Who?"

"Maybe Comanche. A bright flash off a mirror or shiny silver concho just struck me." On his knees, he tried to see the source, and lined up the sun's position to decide that it must be west of them. With the sun nearly at high noon, the glare had to come to him from the west.

"See anything?" she asked in a fear-filled voice.

"No. That's what upsets me." His eyes narrowed against the midday glare, he searched for any sign across the wide horizon beyond the shallow lake. To know they were out there was better than not knowing a thing and having them slipping in to cut his throat. Still, he needed to know how many and who. Then he spotted a rider, and at first thought he wore a hat.

"We've got company coming."

"Who?" she asked, trying to follow his pointing finger. "Oh, I see him."

"I'd say he was white."

"What's he doing out here?"

"That's anyone's guess. But he ain't a Comanche from the sight of his hat. Better make some coffee."

She gathered up her skirts to get up, and paused to look pained at Slocum. "Oh, well, so much for our privacy."

"Yeah, so much for it now."

The man rode a jaded horse. A puncher by dress, Slocum guessed him to be in his forties. He removed his weathered hat, once gray, more black-stained than anything else. A tear was in the brim, and his too-long dark hair fell over his eyes. He swept it back with a coarse-sounding "Morning, ma'am."

"That's Mary and I'm Slocum. Drop down and sit. She's got coffee a-making."

"Ah, Mary, that would be so kind of you. I'm Heck and I ain't had a woman's hand at making coffee in months."

"Where are you headed, Heck?" Slocum asked.

"Ah, just sugar-footing around. Thought I might go see Mexico."

"Know anyone there?"

"Naw, after the war I came home and there was no one there. Our little ranch house was burned to the ground. Three graves marked me mother, father, and sister. Injuns, the neighbors said done it. Nothing left for me to stay around for, you see?"

"Indians?"

"Some say so—some say it was bandits. But it was long over and the grass grew upon their graves. Nothing I could do."

"Oh, that sounds so sad," Mary said, adding ground coffee to her boiling water.

"And it was. So I've been drifting ever since. My feet itch, I guess. Can't stay anywhere too long."

Slocum indicated the ground and both men sat down. "Heck, a man named Paco, Mary, and me have several head of branded cattle we inherited that need to be driven to Sedalia, Missouri."

"Sedalia, huh?"

"Yes, you ever been there?"

"Yeah, or close, with General Sterling Price. We made us a swipe up there about the end of the war."

"I recall hearing about that raid. What's it like?"

"Rolling country. Lots of water and grass when I was up there. But them folks ain't going to hug you being a Reb and all. See, Missouri had two sides. One South, one North. I reckon they won't be beholding to no graybacks coming through again."

"That's the railhead, isn't it? As far west as the tracks go?"

Heck combed his hair back through his fingers and nodded. "Still, it ain't no place I'd go."

"Cattle ain't worth nothing in Texas. They say in Saint Louis or Chicago, they're worth real money."

"Aye, but getting them there."

"Paco's gone to hire some Mexican vaqueros. I need eighty mustangs caught and broke. Cattle gathered and started north to winter so we're ready to hit the market as soon as we can get them there."

"All that costs money." He narrowed his eyelids and looked around. "This place ain't no headquarters for a big ranch."

"It's a cow camp. We've got lots of head branded and yoked to tame them. Now some bandits shot up the crew that the colonel had. We buried them and never found his body. So Mary, Paco, and I inherited the deal."

"But it takes lots of supplies—"

"We have that. I can offer you ten percent of the deal if we make it."

Heck looked dismayed by the offer. "You know how far Sedalia is from here?"

"Months at ten to fifteen miles a day." Slocum said as Mary brought tin cups and the pot. "The deal is if we can get there. There'll be money to pay back our credit, the crew, and have some in our pockets."

"I guess Mexico can wait. Where do we start?"

"Roping and gentling down twenty horses after we grab a bite to eat. They're in a trap up the way."

"Twenty horses?" Heck swallowed hard.

Slocum noticed the silver buttons on his sweat-stained leather vest. They were the cause of the flash. "Won't take more'n a couple of days."

"I've got beans heating," Mary said, and smiled. "I can put on more for supper. They should be done when we get back."

"Are you his missus?"

She shook her head. "I'm a runaway Comanche captive. They—Paco and Slocum rescued me. My family is dead too."

"Yes, ma'am. That's a real sad common word these days."

"We have some sugar somewhere in our packs," she offered as he blew on the hot coffee.

He waved her off. "It's good enough, and I am grateful to both of you."

"We'll see how long that lasts." Slocum laughed over the rim of his cup.

Heck nodded, busy sipping coffee.

On fresh horses, they roped and castrated the captured horses that afternoon. Mary came with the hot branding iron each time and they put the colonel's A2X brand on the horses' left shoulders. It was hard work, with plenty of hot sun baking man and beast, stinking brand smoke to coil up Slocum's nose, and the blood from the surgery dried on his fingers tightening them as he worked. All the horses left wore drag ropes; heads down, they stood around and blew wearily in the dust, including the former stud.

"You were lucky to get those other grown males in with the herd," Heck said as they squatted in the dying sun admiring their work. "They're usually outcasts off alone."

"We'd probably not have rounded them up, but the stallion took a wide course and they must have fell in with the bunch."

Heck nodded and shook his head. "We'll need lots more luck to ever get eighty horses."

"Hell, we're a quarter of the way there. Let's go home."

Mary nodded, and they led their saddle horses out of the enclosure. Then they trotted in the twilight for camp. Shadows began to swath the land and the night insects started to chirp. Slocum decided the new man would earn his salt. Heck could rope and ride. As they headed home, Slocum felt better at having him along.

The next day the real work began. Horse-breaking proved tougher despite the horses' surgery—they still kicked and fought being saddled. The worst ones were tied down on a canvas sheet for a few hours. Slocum and Heck took turns going over and sitting on the prone ponies to show them they couldn't escape. Besides being strange to the horses, this took some of the wild sap out of them like the yokes did to cattle.

Some horses could be ridden easily on the third day. Others still had spurts of bucking that jarred their riders in stiff-legged landings on springs of steel. But as the days passed, all the horses could be ridden, even the chestnut stud.

After a week, they finally led the horses back to camp and hobbled them. Slocum had begun his horse tally book. Each had a name. Baldy was the bald-faced horse. They called the former stallion General Lee, the dun Dun, a bay horse Star for the spot on his forehead. A big leggy red roan was named Sarge for some red-haired Irish sergeant Heck knew in the war. Toby, Big John, Rafter, soon they all had names in Slocum's book. Counting all the horses they had, they were up to thirty-six.

The next day, they scouted for more. Topping a rise, Slocum saw three multicolored horses raising their heads from grazing. His hand went for his gun butt in the holster. Indians!

"There's three more," Heck hissed. "There's half a dozen of them!"

"Those are buffalo-hunting horses," Slocum said, anxious about their situation because Mary was along with them. He studied how the rising wind lifted the horses' braided manes and how they watched the three riders more curious than afraid of them.

She pushed her bay in close to the two men. "See the owners anywhere?"

"No, and it makes the skin on my neck itch," Slocum said. "Heck, you circle west and look for any footprints. We can't be lucky enough to find six broke horses."

"Keep the likes of your six-gun handy," Heck said and rode west.

"I will. Mary, you stay close too." Slocum bent over in

the saddle looking for any sign of footprints. Making a quarter circle around the animals, he spotted none.

"They came from the west." Heck pointed as he rode over. "No sign of anything but them."

Mary nodded. "No sign here either."

"Catch one," Slocum said to him. "And the rest will follow. Mary and I can herd them."

For a long moment, Heck looked at him. "What if they want them back?"

"They come looking for them, they would find us up here anyway."

"Guess you're right." Heck shook out a loop. "Put 'em in the tally book, boss." Then he rode off after one.

With the six new ones in the herd, the riders rested the next day, taking baths, shaving, and washing their clothes. Some tall clouds gathered in the west so the sunset was painted red on the high tops, but no rain came. Might have rained forty miles west or so the way lightning danced on the horizon that evening. Heck was gone off to sleep somewhere on the other side of camp, and Slocum and Mary were sitting on their bedroll in each other's arms, kissing and watching the far-off storm.

"Nice to be clean for once," she said softly as he gently felt her firm breast through the blouse's material.

"Yes, I'm plumb disinterested in getting dirty again."

She chuckled softly. "Oh, well, we don't need to get all sweaty and worked up then tonight."

"Who said that—" He quickly smothered her mouth with his and forced her down on the blankets.

Giggling underneath him, she tore at his pants to open them. Fondling his rising erection, she grinned at him over her discovery. Then, gathering her skirt up in a wad to her waist and exposing her bare legs, she raised her knees on both sides of him and threw her head back. "Make me sweaty."

And he did.

It was past midnight when he awoke and listened. It was no coyote out there making that call. They had company. He needed to get word to Heck in his bedroll across camp. He pressed a finger to her mouth to silence her when she stirred, and he whispered, "Comanches are here. I've got to warn Heck."

She nodded as he placed the pistol in her hands with a soft: "Five shots. Use them wisely."

She nodded, and he had his boots on and was on the run, staying as low as he could with the Spencer rifle in his right hand and still make time. He reached Heck's bedroll and squatted beside him.

"Best get up. We've got company."

Heck was instantly awake and never hesitated pulling on his boots. "How many?"

"I ain't sure. I think I've heard three."

"There's one," Heck said after the yipping went off to the south of them.

"Damn sure no coyote," Slocum said in a low voice.

"Not a very good call either."

"No. I'm going back to Mary. You take care."

"He ain't no better than that, I might sneak up on him."

"That's your call. Be careful."

"I will." Heck rubbed the back of his neck. "I like this old world too well to take many chances."

Slocum left him to join Mary. He dropped down on his haunches beside where she sat on the bedroll with the Colt in her hand. No sign of the would-be raiders—then he heard the rustle of a rawhide sole on some twigs and made a shushing sound to her. He eased the hammer back on the rifle as the figure with a headband and a lance came into Slocum's starlit view.

With a steady aim, he squeezed the trigger and the barrel belched orange fire and smoke. There was a sound like a thud on a watermelon and the lance flew into the ground before the buck. Slocum's second shot staggered him some more and he went down.

At the sharp cry to his left, Slocum rose to his feet. It was not Heck's voice and he couldn't see anything. Two figures were running in the starlight toward the west.

"Stay here," Slocum said to Mary, and took off running after them. Anyone that escaped only meant more would return. Comanche were the poorest runners of any tribe, but those two had a good start and their short bow legs were churning ground under the stars.

Soon Heck, armed with a pistol in his fist, was running beside him.

"Can't let 'em—get away." Heck huffed out the words.

"Right . . ."

One of the raiders stopped and turned as if to fire an arrow at them. On the run, Slocum took him out with a single rifle shot. The Indian dropped his bow and fell on the ground crying in pain. Both Slocum and Heck topped the rise, and Slocum saw one of the raiders already on his mount, another trying to get aboard his frightened horse.

Heck deliberately shot the pony under the one in the saddle. The paint horse reared, screaming in pain. Then the horse fell over backward before the Comanche could get clear of him and mashed its rider. The last one, unable to mount, charged Slocum and Heck in suicidal fashion, and ran into a volley of their hot lead that stopped him in his tracks.

"Had to shoot the horse or he'd been gone," Heck said.

"Yeah." Slocum nodded that he understood. Their lives depended on those young bucks never returning to their camp and reporting this night. Revenge for their death would have been something kinfolk would have needed to attend to. Slocum turned his ear to the night—nothing but a hoot owl and the hard-breathing horse struggling on the ground.

"We better be damn sure they're dead," Heck said, and Slocum agreed.

"I'll check on the two back there and see about Mary," Slocum said.

"Fine. I'll be damn sure we've got these two."

Slocum had not gone far until he heard two shots. One no doubt was for the horse—number two the injured Comanche on the ground. Tough world they lived in, but there was no room for mistakes in this business. When he knelt in the starlight and checked for a pulse below the ear of the Comanche who had charged them, he found he was dead.

Mary came running to meet him. "You—you all right?"

"Yes. Heck is too."

"I—I heard shots."

He hugged her shoulder. "They're all dead. Don't worry."

"Oh, I was so scared." She trembled under his left arm as he held her against his chest.

"They won't bother anyone ever again."

"Good. I'll make some coffee. I don't suppose any of us can sleep after this."

"Good idea. We'll have to bury them."

She nodded and gathering her skirt, rushed off to camp ahead of him.

He looked back in the night's glow and waited for Heck, who was coming.

"How many horses?" he asked Heck when he caught up.

"Oh, I think they had a couple extra. Maybe stolen ranch horses."

Slocum clapped him on the shoulder. "Beats having to break them."

"Damn sure does." Heck chuckled. "Don't guess them vaqueros will care. A horse is a horse to them."

Slocum nodded. Where was Paco? He was overdue to be back. Something was keeping him—either pussy or high water. And Slocum doubted high water was the problem.

After breakfast, they buried the four in a common grave and rode their horses back and forth over it to hide as much sign as possible. They'd gained two cap-and-ball pistols and a single-shot trapdoor rifle with a pouch of ammo. No doubt stolen from one of the Indians' victims on the war trail. Also two good saddles and pads. When they gathered their new horses, two big stout brown horses showed collar marks. Slocum was pleased. They'd make a team for the cart. The new horse tally came to forty-four.

"This is a damn sight easier than breaking them," Heck

said, and laughed aloud when Slocum wrote the new ones down in his tally book.

"Just so folks don't think we stole them, we'll be all right."

Heck took off his hat and checked the midday sun. "You have a point."

"It could happen." Slocum tucked the tally book and lead pencil in his saddlebag. "We've got more worries than that if Paco don't come back soon."

"Guess you're right."

10

Slocum heard the bells first. He was scouting cattle in a wide draw when he first heard them, and turned his left ear toward the ringing sound. Pushing his horse to the rise, he could see a caravan of carts, horses, streamers fluttering, even some cattle and sheep being driven along with them. Was that Paco? He short-loped the bay toward them, seeing the familiar sombrero of the rider on the black lead horse. It was no doubt his overdue partner, but he must have brought his entire village along. What would they do with all of them? This was a cattle drive—not a pilgrimage.

"Ha, *mi amigo*. Bet you thought I was never coming."

Slocum nodded, noticing several attractive women on foot walking beside the carts. "I thought you went for vaqueros, not families."

"Oh, it is hard to get men to come." He shrugged under his thick vest. "So I brought some women. That helped. Some of them can ride too. Some are only good for fucking, but what the hell, we can use them too." He laughed aloud. "You have any trouble?"

"Some Comanches dropped in."

Paco grinned and gave a nod to Heck, who was riding up to meet them. "Who is he?"

"Our new partner. He's a good man. Name's Heck. We have forty-four horses."

"Oh, you two have been very busy. I brought two dozen. A man owed me money in Mexico. I took his horses as payment."

"Good. We're close to the number we need. We have to unyoke the rest of the cattle and head north. No rain and the feed is getting short around here."

"Good. How is the señora?"

"Fine, she'll be excited."

"About me coming back?"

"No, she'll have some women to talk to."

Paco laughed. "There are ten men and two boys and two of the women who can ride like sandburs. The other women are camp helpers."

Heck reined up his bald-faced horse and blinked at the caravan. "What did he bring?"

"A fiesta to take to Missouri."

His hat in his hand, Heck shook his head in disbelief at what he saw. "Hell, there are even sheep."

"To eat," Paco said. "The sheep you can cook them for one or two meals before they spoil. They are cheap too."

"Paco, meet Heck."

The two men rode in close and shook hands. A friendly exchange of words and Paco said, "Ah, you would like Rosa. She is a good one."

"Hell—" Heck scratched his rumpled hair looking after the women. "I'd like anything." They all laughed.

The camp was soon bustling. Slocum met several of the new men. Their names flew by him as he organized the group to repair saddles. Paco had brought several extra old saddles, and some of the men had their own. Many needed severe work, and Slocum sent the youngest boy, Tomas, to Rio Frio to get copper rivets, girths, and a couple of leather hides to finish the job. There were enough hulls, if they could be repaired, that the crew would all have saddles.

The women butchered a sheep and began to cook it on a

spit. Two of the vaqueros on horseback dragged in mesquite to keep the fire going. Slocum had spoken to Mary twice since they arrived, and she sounded in good spirits over the women. By sundown, all but the worst rigs were fixed and the crew was ready to eat the frijoles, rich mesquite-smelling sheep, and tortillas.

Tomas returned and Slocum went to meet the boy. He took the two hides wrapped in a roll from him and the youth jumped down.

"How did it go?"

"Fine. He gave me some candy."

"You had a wonderful day then?"

"*Sí*, Señor Slocum." The boy was busy undoing the latigos to remove the saddle. "Oh, this is a wonderful horse."

"He single-foots."

"It is very fast too. Oh, the man sent you a message." He reached inside his shirt and handed Slocum a paper damp with the youth's sweat.

Slocum set the leather down beside his leg, turned the note toward the last light in the west, and read the pencil scrawl.

Slocum,

*Beware. I have word that Matt is close by in Mexico.
Herman Goeserman*

How close? Slocum had all the responsibility for this herd, for all these people. No way he could simply haul up stakes and go look for that killer. Settling with Matt would have to wait until the drive was over. In the meantime, maybe some Good Samaritan might do the world a big favor and send Matt to hell.

"News?" Mary asked, joining them.

"Goeserman sent a note that Matt is somewhere in Mexico."

"Close by?"

He shook his head to dismiss her concern and picked up

the roll of leather. "We don't have time to mess with him. We need these cattle unyoked and moved to more grass and water."

"We can start in the morning," Paco said, joining them.

"Goeserman wrote that Matt is in Mexico."

"Ah, I would like to kill him."

"That makes two of us." Slocum shook his head. "We've got too much at stake here. His funeral can wait."

"What will we do next?"

"Start roping and unyoking cattle."

Paco nodded as they walked to the campfire. "*Sí,* that will be a big job, but we have the horses."

"And the vaqueros."

"Oh, *sí,* they are good ropers."

"Sunup let's get started."

One of the men, named Jerome, came and took the leather. "I can fix the rest of the saddles."

"Good, the two boys can collect the good yokes with a cart. They might have some value," Slocum said.

"Come and eat." The woman called Matilda waved them toward the food. An ample-bodied woman in her thirties, she supervised the cooking.

Slocum had to agree the slow-cooked mesquite-flavored sheep was delicious. He sat cross-legged beside Mary and ate until he felt ready to burst. Much better than any fare they'd managed to rustle up.

"I would hire her," Mary said, wiping her mouth on a kerchief.

"We may get fat on this run." Slocum smiled and listened to Paco talking in Spanish to the crew. He made teams of the men and the two women dressed in vaquero leather clothing. Both were slender and short, but they looked very athletic in their moves. Estelle and Vonda Santiago were sisters. Their hair was cut short and they might have been taken for boys at first glance. Large sombreros rested on their shoulders and their skills as ranch hands, Slocum figured, were not to be underestimated.

The men were all in their late teens to twenties. In the fire's reflection, they looked anxious to get this business under way.

"How far is Sedalia?" one asked Paco, who turned back to Slocum for the answer.

Slocum wiped his calloused hand over his whisker-bristled mouth and shook his head as if uncertain. "Three to four months away. That's after the spring grass breaks out."

The answer satisfied the man, who nodded in approval to the others around the fire. Guitars and fiddles began to liven up the night. Soon couples were dancing. Matilda came and asked Mary if she could dance with Slocum.

"Of course."

Slocum danced slowly with her in the dirt, circling around the red light. They went around smoothly as if on a polished dance floor.

"Where's my partner Heck?" he asked her under his breath. "You seen him?"

She looked up at him and grinned as if slightly embarrassed. "Oh, he and Rosa are having their own fandango."

"So I ain't lost him." Slocum laughed softly and took a better hitch on his hand around her waist. They danced away in easy circles.

"No problem," Matilda said, and looked up at him. "The señora? Paco said the Comanches kidnapped her."

"Mary's a fine lady. She lost her husband and son too."

Matilda nodded as he swung her around to the music. "It is not a good time. Both of my husbands were killed."

"Comanche?"

"Banditos the first, and maybe Indians killed the second one."

He looked off into the starlit night. The killing never stopped. The war was over and another begun—maybe more than one. The thought made his guts roil as the soft music filled the night and he spun the firm-bodied Matilda around in a circle.

Maybe, maybe they would soon be moving cattle.

11

The help worked wonders. In three days they had removed most of the yokes and a herd was established. Slocum had never seen such work before from Mexicans, and they enjoyed it. Riding straight-backed in their saddles and recoiling their lariats, they rode for the next cows wearing yokes, laughing and teasing all day about a hock that someone missed catching or a fighting steer that tried to hook a man on foot with his horn tip. The two boys gathered a growing pile of the wooden yokes.

Horses bucked and threw a few, but most riders were learning fast. The tougher broncs were assigned to the better riders like Montag and Felipe. Most of the jump was gone from them after a few tough days roping and hauling around big steers. The week drew to a close, and the outfit was ready to make a new camp north of the present one. This left some of the less experienced men as herders to hold the cattle in a bunch and eventually move them up the line.

Slocum, Mary, and the boy Tomas took the four team horses they picked out of the remuda to Rio Frio. All had shoulder scars from being under collars and harnesses—they also acted like teams. Two horses that had been worked a lot soon became paired. Obviously stolen or strayed from some operation, they'd be the best ones, Slocum felt.

Goeserman had found a second cart, and they improvised
to hitch it behind the first. The storekeeper even discovered
some solid sun-bleached bows so the rigs could be covered
with a tarp. Mary and the women sewed openings in each
end that could be shut with a cord. Then, with a flap to go
over the cooking area, Goeserman produced some peeled
cedar posts with iron pegs driven in the ends to use for corners. Mary smiled all day working on her tasks.

"Won't we be the outfit with all this!"

Slocum stopped and nodded. "I ain't sure what it's cost-
ing us." He glanced toward the store. "But it'll sure be better
than some things I've been on."

The work was completed by dark, and Gresalda invited
the three of them to dinner. She fussed over Tomas.

"Where is your family?"

"In Sonora, Señora."

"Do you miss them?"

"Oh, sometimes my *madre,* but Señor Slocum he feeds us
good."

"He does?"

"*Sí,* I have never been hungry since I got to his camp."

"That's wonderful."

"No, Señora, I thank God every day for him."

"And you can use that too," Mary said in a whisper to
Slocum.

He nodded and smiled. Eating every day was a luxury to
many people including, many times, himself, going back to
the war even. He could recall a small white hen he'd caught
in a burned-out farm. A treasure overlooked somehow by
past invaders. How he and his corporal had picked and
dressed it, then slowly cooked it over a hot fire on a
makeshift spit. Best chicken he ever ate, including his own
mother's fried chicken, which drew saliva to his mouth when
he thought about the flavor. That particular meal came after
two days of grazing on watercress they'd found in various
clear spring runoffs as they scouted the countryside in
search of Yankee outfits. The waterborne plants were not the
most nutritious or filling, so the fowl they shared that night

in the smoldering ruins tasted like pure manna from heaven.

With daylight breaking, the two hitched teams hit the collars to move the tandem carts loaded with supplies. Slocum rode with a lead on the left horse, Mary on the right one. That way, if the teams spooked, they couldn't run off. Slocum and Mary could hold them back and protect the supplies and food in the wagons.

An anxious Tomas held the reins and looked very pale. Nonetheless, he had no intention of disappointing his boss, and with white knuckles held the reins for the four horses like a true stage driver.

"Ready, Tomas?" Slocum asked

"*Sí, patrón.*"

"Cluck to them softly at first."

The boy made a soft sound and the lead team began to dance. Slocum nodded to Mary, and then he waved to the storekeeper and others on the porch. The outfit was off for Missouri, or at least in that direction. He didn't know about the rest—time would tell.

Tomas soon was driving the team, but Slocum kept Diamond alongside the leader in case anything spooked them. He nodded for Mary to toss the lead rope over the other team's leader.

"They should be fine," he said. "I don't want them to run off with all our food on board."

She agreed and smiled. "Going great."

"Yes." For the moment anyway.

Past noon, they were in camp and the women ran over to examine the supplies he'd brought back. He dismounted and began to unhitch the first team, loosening the tugs from the singletree. Mary held the reins while Tomas undid his tugs and neck yoke. When the horses were unhitched, they began to strip off the harnesses and collars, careful to pile the gear in place so it was ready to be reused on the same horses.

"Will all that food get us to Missouri?" Matilda asked him under her breath as he put down the second set of gear.

He straightened and reset his felt hat and looked hard at her. "We'll probably need more."

"No problem, Señor. I meant it must be a long way up there."

"Far enough."

"I will use it with care."

"Good, it costs many dollars. I must pay the storekeeper back when we sell the cattle."

"Señor?"

"Yes?" Mary brought him his horse.

"God be with you." Then the woman crossed herself.

"And you too, Matilda." He swung into the saddle. "We'll all need his help before we can get there."

"What was wrong?" Mary asked when they were out of earshot.

"She merely wondered how far away Sedalia was and how to ration out the food."

"Oh, I see. She is such a caring person."

"Yes, let's find Paco and Heck. We need this carnival on the road."

Mary laughed. "I thought we were gypsies."

"Them too."

"All those flags and bells. Sounded like them coming in that day."

Slocum chuckled, but he was watching a large thunderhead that had been building all day in the southwest. It had reached serious downpour heights and looked headed for them later. Great bilious clouds were stacking higher and higher in the sky, mushrooming in rapid enough fashion to make him uneasy.

"You head back for camp and tell them to tie everything down. We're going to have lightning, thunder, high winds, and hail, plus flooding rain in a few hours."

She blinked at him, reining up her horse. "What will you do?"

"Try to keep the cattle herd together."

"Oh, Slocum be careful. They—they'll stampede."

"It may test all of us this evening."

She reined her horse back around. "I'll do the best I can at camp. You be careful."

He nodded in approval, watched her race off, and then he turned Diamond westward. He needed to find the herd and get them on the move before the storm struck. The ominous growing clouds made him hurry.

He discovered Paco and Heck unyoking another pair of cattle.

"You get the supplies all right?" Heck asked, coiling up his lariat and heading for his horse.

"Got everything I asked for and more. But those clouds out there are brewing up a goose drowneder." Slocum gave a head toss toward the clouds.

"What should we do, amigo?" Paco asked, sitting his dun horse and looking out of the corner of his eye at the clouds as he recoiled his lariat.

"Line them up and move them in a line until we're out from under it."

"Why do that?" Heck asked.

"You can never hold a herd in a bad storm. They'd break and run every way. In a column, they'll be closer to us when we go look for the stragglers."

"Never thought of that." Heck shook his head. "I've got lots to learn about cattle driving."

"We all do. Paco, get the two best riders for swing men. Maybe we can find a lead steer in this mess to bell."

"Bell?" Heck asked.

"Yes, I made some cattle drives during the war and picked up some pointers. Most drives have a bell lead steer so the cattle will follow him. I helped some drovers in Mississippi drive some Texas cattle to the troops during the war."

"Where do we get one?" Heck asked.

"I think, we survive this, we'll have us one that shows up as the leader."

"Good, I'll be looking."

"How many head have we got?"

"Paco and I think close to three hundred," Heck said.

"A good-size bunch to start on. Get those two and we'll talk swing riders with them," Slocum said to Paco, who tore off to find them.

"I'll get all the riders north of here," Heck said.

"Good idea," Slocum said. "I'll ride south, get them, and meet back here."

Slocum parted with Heck and short-loped Diamond, standing up looking for any sign of more riders. The growl of the distant storm floating across the land made his stomach roil. They needed to hurry or else they might lose a large portion of the herd.

At the top of a rise, he spotted two riders working a yoked team. The Santiago sisters had one steer heeled and down. The girls looked like twins—slender bodies dressed in buckskin pants. One girl shook the head holder loose on the steer on his knees until he came free, then began to work on the downed one. It came harder, and the critter began to flop and bellow like she was killing him. Holding the yoke upright, she wrestled to free him, but it looked hopeless until Slocum drew up short and it came loose.

The freed steer jumped to his feet and took off for far west Texas with the other one on his heels. Both girls were laughing as they coiled up their ropes. Slenderly built as young boys and ready to remount, the Santiago sisters looked a little shocked at his approach.

"Any other riders around?" he asked, looking over the country.

The one with the beauty mark on her cheek, Vonda, shook her head. "No, Señor. Paco sent us to find these."

He pointed to the towering storm. "That's going to blow in some hail and bad weather. We need to get the cattle on the move so they don't stampede."

"Where will we take them?" Estelle asked, getting on her paint horse in one leap off the ground. Both girls rode buffalo ponies and were busy tying their lariats on their saddles.

"North—that's where we want to end up. Find Paco and he can tell you more."

"What about those two steers that ran away?" Vonda asked with a head toss toward the fleeing pair.

"Get them later. We better ride." The air was still, hot, and it was hard to even take a breath.

He led the way and they raced for the herd. When he topped the ridge, he could see that Heck, Paco, and the two swing riders had the herd heading out. His plan might work.

"Drive the ones that break out of the herd back in," he shouted at the girls as the first cold blast struck his face. The girls were gone in a flash and he joined the drag riders.

Spooked by the growing thunder and flashes of lightning, the herd was becoming hard to hold. He could see that the riders were doing a good job in the face of such a disturbance crashing into them. The motion of heading out soon occupied the animals, and they fell in line, rapidly moving in a great string stretched over a quarter mile long toward the North Star.

A huge shadow like a giant hovering hawk swept over them. Slocum undid his slicker and managed to get it on as large icy drops struck him. The incisive downpour soon shortened his vision. Ice pellets bounced off his hat brim and shoulders. Some hit hard enough to sting, but the raucous sound of the wind and hail deafened even the confused cattle's bawling and horn-knocking. A stream ran off the brim of his hat like a waterfall and he knew if the rain continued for long at that rate, the draws would soon be rivers. Still, he could see cattle on his right in a long line following the leader and not scattering to hell and back.

Then, through the sheets of rain, he spotted a figure on foot, looking to dodge any cattle and find a ride. Slocum pushed Diamond in close and put out his arm for the half-drowned puncher. He was surprised when one of the sisters leaped on behind him.

"You all right?"

"*Sí*, my horse went down. May have broke his leg. You seen Vonda?" she shouted over the roar, hugging tight to him.

"No. But she'll be fine."

"I know, but she'll be looking for me."

"We'll find her—" His words were cut off by the boom of thunder over their heads.

Lightning flashed and blinded him for a moment, then more rumbling. It wasn't going to slack off for a while. But the bawling cattle were at least, for the most part, getting in line. His rider clinging to him, he pushed on parallel to what he could see of the herd in the deluge.

Slocum charged over a rise, and several steers on his right went end over end. Circling back, he watched the confusion and jamming. The pileup threatened to break up the column. He booted Diamond toward them and he and Estelle screamed and waved the cattle back into the line. It worked, and he reined up Diamond to watch the column flying past and even jumping over the downed ones.

Satisfied, he pushed Diamond on in a hard trot.

"I thought they would break up there," she said, leaning forward to be heard over the racket.

"It could have happened. They want to be in the safety of the herd if you encourage them."

"I'm learning today. We've worked lots of cattle, but never in a storm like this."

Then as fast as it came, the clouds moved to the northeast and the shiny stream of sleek cattle slowed to a walk. Wet riders began to reappear in their places along the snaking line of longhorns. Time to circle them back, Slocum decided, and set Diamond in a lope for the front.

He slid Diamond to a stop at Paco. "Turn them back in a big circle. We need to let them graze some here and count our crew."

"You have one, I see."

"She's fine. But she's worried she lost her buffalo horse. We'll go back and find out."

"I'll have them circle and spread them out, *mi amigo*. You seen Heck?"

Slocum frowned. "No, but he's somewhere out here."

"I'll go look too."

"I hope they made it all right in camp."

"Mary there?"

"Yes, I sent her back to help them buckle down."

"Man, that was a bad one." Paco looked off at the tall cloud formation in the sky moving away from them.

"We may see worse."

Paco laughed. "I guess there is no way to make easy money, is there?"

"Rob banks, I guess."

Paco shook his head. "Oh, they catch you, that would be worse."

Slocum agreed and rode off to find his passenger's horse.

Near the site of the wreck, he spotted a broken-legged steer hobbling around on three legs and bawling. The women could make jerky out of him. "I'll send the boys back to butcher him."

"*Sí.* I thought there would be more," Estelle said, scooting around to make her seat behind him.

"We haven't seen all of them yet."

"I sure liked that horse—Diablo. I'll hate it if he broke his leg."

"He may have only sprained it."

"I hope so. I see now how those Comanche can ride in and shoot a buffalo from off a horse. He has no fear."

"People say they are the greatest horsemen on the plains."

"If they have horses like him, it wouldn't be hard."

"There." He pointed to the saddled paint horse standing head down, slick with the rainwater dripping off him.

She bounded off and with her hand out, spoke softly, headed toward the horse when he threw up his head. Acting undecided, he stood his ground until she swept up the reins and he snorted at her. She lifted the reins and he stepped forward, and a wave of relief swept her smooth coffee-colored face as he circled her with his head high.

"Go easy on him a few days. He may have sprained it in the fall. Looks great to me. Lead him in."

She ran over and gave Slocum the reins. "Oh, thank the Virgin Mary." Jumping on behind him in a bound, she crossed herself. "Mother of God . . ."

Her sister soon came short-loping over the rise from the east on her black piebald with a bald face. She slid him up short of Diamond.

"You are all right?" Vonda asked her sister with a frown.

"I'm fine. So is Diablo. He fell and I lost him in the rain."

"Any of the other riders get hurt that you know about?" Slocum asked Vonda, looking over the greasewood shining with water.

"Grande Juan's horse broke a leg, but he is all right."

Slocum nodded to Estelle. "You can ride double with her. I better get a cart and butcher that steer back there."

"Gracias, patrón," Estelle said, and slipped off Diamond's rump.

The two sisters fell into talking about the storm as he short-loped off to camp. On the go, he shrugged off the slicker, which was getting too hot to wear in the rising heat. Relieved at his first sight of the camp, he rode on in to be met by an anxious-looking Mary.

"Everyone is all right, but we thought we might blow away. How are the others?" Mary asked.

"I haven't seen Heck. Grande Juan lost his horse and Estelle took a spill. She and her horse are fine." He spotted Tomas. "You and Juan hitch up a cart. We have a steer with a broken leg that we need to butcher."

"Sí, patrón." The youth shouted to his cohort and they rushed off for the horses.

"Rosa and Gato can go with you," Matilda said to Slocum. "They know how to butcher. Help me get them some knives and a saw." She stopped. "And make them be careful with the hide. No holes in it. We can always use the leather."

"I will," Slocum said. He swung down, pulled his pants out of his crotch, and stretched his tight back muscles. Been a real close call. Their losses could have been much worse.

"Bring me back the skull too," Matilda said, coming out with her hands full. "I want his brains to tan it with."

"Yes, ma'am," Slocum said and chuckled. She wasn't wasting anything.

Rosa looked bored when she came out of the women's tent still dressing herself. Obviously, she had been sleeping. Gato was a small, swarthy girl, perhaps older than she appeared. At the sight of him, she turned away and slid to a place behind the tailgate of the big cart where she could not be seen. With a fearful look in her eyes, she always hung back at the sight of him.

When the boys brought the smaller cart up with one horse in the shafts, Rosa made a face. "Shit! We'll all have to walk home if that steer's meat weighs anything."

"Shut your mouth, girl," Matilda ordered. "You want to walk back home?"

"No, but—"

Matilda, with her hands full of knives and the stones to sharpen them, frowned her into silence. The utensils were stowed in a wooden box, and Matilda told the girls and Tomas she wanted all of her knives back. Juan brought a hatchet to chop the bones. When he put it in the cart, Rosa demanded that he lift her in too.

He bent over and hugged her around the top of her legs. She giggled as he strained and finally, red-faced, the youth hoisted her butt up on the bed of the cart. She teased him with her bare foot while he regained his breath. Gato took no chance at being squeezed by Juan. Like a squirrel, she scrambled up the wheel spokes and into the vehicle, then sat in the front under the spring seat and folded her arms defensively over her small bustline.

Juan jumped on the tailgate and Tomas clucked to the horse. Matilda gave one more order, walking beside the cart, telling them to keep the meat clean. "No sand on it!"

"I'll be back," Slocum said to Mary, still wondering about Heck. Strange he hadn't shown up. Slocum booted Diamond after the cart. The horse dropped his head, blowing hard from being weary. He'd be all right—this would be quick work.

Mary waved and they were off. He recognized Paco coming at a long lope and rode out to meet him.

"What's wrong?"

"Heck is bad hurt. His horse fell and rolled on him. He wants to talk to you."

"Why me?"

Paco shook his head, looking very serious.

"Should we take the cart for him?"

"No." Paco's face showed the seriousness of the matter. "He won't live long."

"Let's ride then."

They raced their horses northward. The soft ground gave under their ponies' hooves and they churned up the land. Slocum had a million questions clouding his mind. What did Heck need to tell him? They sped faster, and soon saw the crew, with their hats off, gathered around a body on the ground. Too late.

Slocum slid to halt, and stepped off even before Diamond stopped. He ran over and fell to his knees beside the crumpled Heck. They'd made a bed of their saddle blankets for him. A small smile was in the corner of Heck's mouth, and he coughed deep, staring bleary-eyed up at Slocum.

"Key in my boot—safe deposit box in the Texas State Bank . . . Fort Worth—you—you—can have it all . . ."

"Heck? Heck?"

But Heck's head had slumped to the side. His blue eyes glazed over. He'd gone on to his own outfit. Slocum swept his hat off and looked hard at the clear azure sky overhead. Never even knew his last name. Left him something in a safety deposit box in Fort Worth—what was it? *Damn life could be tough for the living.*

12

The funeral for Heck was at sunrise. Among his few things, Slocum had found a letter addressed to Heck Allen. The letter was about a deed and came from a lawyer in Dallas, who said Heck's claim had been upheld and the land was his—but there was no deed. Maybe there was something in the deposit box to answer Slocum's questions.

"Dear Father," Slocum began, "we're sending our pard Heck Allen to your place in the sky. We don't know much about Heck. He always carried his part of the load with us. You couldn't ask more than that of any man. And he sure treated everyone in the outfit square. We lost him, Lord, with all of us trying hard to keep the herd intact. Keep him in the palm of your hand, Lord. Amen."

Rosa cried the hardest. Matilda and Vonda had to carry her back to the tent—one girl under each of her arms. Grande Juan, the widest-built man in the outfit, handed Slocum a shovel.

"You toss in the first shovelful. We'll do the rest, Señor."

Afraid to say much himself, Slocum nodded hard, tossed in the first load of dirt, thanked the man, and gave him back the shovel. Mary led Slocum away. Not that there were many places to go. She took him over the rise and they sat side by side on the blanket she spread for them. They listened to some meadowlarks and quail out in the greasewood that smelled more pungent in the rain-washed air.

"He ever say what he'd do with his share from the drive?" Mary was rattling some small rocks from one fist to the other.

"Only thing he ever said to me was he was going to Mexico and stopped by our camp."

"He didn't have much money on him. Thirty dollars? Something close to that. How far could he go?"

"He wasn't worried. Never asked for any money when I hired him."

On his back, Slocum stretched out and shook his head. "There's a secret there. We may never learn the answer." He rolled over on his side and propped his head up with a crooked arm. "Shame, wish I'd asked him more."

"That key you got out of his boot might be the answer."

Slocum agreed, wondering how all the pieces fit.

She scooted down and lay on her back beside him. When she turned enough to look over at him, a knowing grin spread over her face. "I didn't forget the blanket."

He reached over and rubbed her tight stomach under the blouse. "No, you did good."

"I figured you needed a powerful distraction."

"I can sure use one." He looked down into her brown eyes and smiled.

"Good. So could I."

He turned to her and pulled up her skirt until his hand was underneath it feeling her silky leg. She moved closer to him as he worked his way to the top of her thighs. Soon his hand cupped her mound and the stiff pubic hair. Her legs fell apart and he moved to kiss her as his finger sought the seam. She raised her knees and spread them further apart in the bright sunshine. The tip of his middle finger teased her clit. It began to swell, and his actions shortened her breath. From head to toe, her entire body began to tremble in passion's arms.

Her mouth fell open and she began to moan. She reached down to clutch his hand to recover her breath. Then, swallowing deep, she released him with a shudder. His probing finger soon found her cunt and slipped through the lubricated gates.

He began to ream her tight ring, and her soft moans turned into sharper cries and she pulled him to her in desperation.

"Now! Now!"

He fought down his pants to his knees and moved over her. His near-rigid dick swung like a long thick bamboo pole. Filled with need, he guided the nose in her and she shouted, "Oh, yes!"

His butt yearned to be as deep as he could go inside her. His knees were confined by his pants—there was no time to remove them—only drive on and on. The walls inside her began to contract. In wild abandonment, she tossed her head and clutched him. Harder, deeper, deeper, until the nose of his dick reached the bottom and she cried out. As she arched her back for him, he felt the explosion in his tubes that burned like fire going out the skintight head that felt blown apart by the action. They collapsed in utter fatigue. The wind blew over them as they half-slept in each other's arms still connected.

In a while, they awoke side by side with him still inside her. With a grin at his discovery, he began to pump his half-hard dick into her. She pulled him over on top of her again and widened her legs for his deeper entry. He pounded away until at last the needles in his butt became sharp hot injections and he came in a great surge.

"I was married three years," she said, sitting up to straighten her clothing. "We had this—but never . . . Can I tell you the truth—I'm so ashamed of it."

"I won't tell anyone." He lay on his back rebuttoning his pants.

"One of those Comanche boys was the first one in my life ever made me drunk doing it."

"Shame, wasn't it?"

"Oh, I about went crazy. How could I? Me enjoying an Indian raping me. He wasn't much more than fifteen. He didn't have a big—organ either. Oh—" She used her hand to sweep the hair back from her forehead and shook her head about to cry. "God, is that so bad?"

He hugged her tight. "Why question it? A boy woke up the woman in you."

"But it was rape. He never kissed me. All he wanted was my body."

"Still, he woke something inside you."

"What is it? That first night with you—you did it to me and I thanked God that night that more than a savage could make me feel like that."

Slocum shook his head. "There is something lies inside most all women, and if a man can kindle the right fire in her, she'll glow."

"No, it's more than that. It's fire and brimstone. It's being so dizzy that you're drunk. Wantonly, I mean, you do it—oh, I recall John had a mare once in heat and she went crazy. That afternoon, he finally took her to the neighbor's stallion and he bred her three times. John was worried the stud horse might die he got so exhausted, but she came home switching her tail for more. Wanted more, can you imagine?"

"What about you?"

She wiggled on the blanket and laughed. "I can't get enough."

He kissed her and raised up to look around. "We better go to camp and join the rest of them."

"Oh, well—"

He pulled her to her feet.

Matilda served them some fire-braised loin cut off the steer and frijoles. When it was washed down with some fresh coffee, Slocum began to feel alive again. The lawyer's letter and key secured in his saddlebags, he went back to work riding Roan. The former stud horse acted up some under the saddle, but soon struck off in a fast trot.

An hour later, he found Paco looking over the herd. He reined the big horse up. Roan gave a sharp cry at Paco's gelding, and it backed away from the sharp challenge before Paco could stop it.

"Whoa, stupid," Slocum said and set Roan down hard with the bosal. "How's it going?"

"We've started unyoking up here. Must have added a hundred head today. It's going good."

"We need to get all the cattle we can and head north.

There is lots of grass up around Fort Worth if we can't winter them at Mason."

"How many head do we need?" Paco asked.

"A thousand would be nice. Eight hundred is all right."

"We get all the yokes off the cattle here and the ones we unyoked up there, we might have that many. What's on your mind, amigo?"

"Comanches. They're all over here. We have women and men to worry about. Closer to the army, we should be better off. I ain't no bluebelly lover, but everyone should be safer there."

Paco agreed. "*Sí,* we got lots of horses, supplies, and women, all the things Comanche wants."

Two days later in the early morning, Slocum rode by Heck's grave and dismounted. The crude cross the boys made from crate lumber wouldn't be there for long. Shifting winds would further erase the signs. With the outfit on the move to the next location, Slocum took a last moment to tell his friend good-bye. He dismounted and dropped the reins at the graveside.

They'd not been together long, but Heck wouldn't be easy to forget. Not many men on the frontier didn't have an agenda of their own that meant they came first and the rest could get by on their own. Not many men didn't scoff at the ideas of others with better ideas of their own. Slocum dropped to his knees recalling the last moments of Heck's life.

"Lord, take good care of him. I want to see him again in that big sky pasture. Amen."

Mary had ridden up, and sat the bay horse a few yards back, waiting for him.

Slocum replaced his hat, set the stirrup, put a boot in it, and swung on board. He gave her a nod that he was ready.

"Guess you've lost many good friends. War and all," she said softly, riding beside him.

"Too many." *Way too many good ones.*

13

The cattle gathering went smoothly the next few weeks. The rain had filled many natural tanks, and the new green growth mixed well with the dry bunchgrass. His tally book boasted nine hundred head. No sign of any Comanche. The notion that they had not been around made Slocum a little easier. But not a bloody sundown went by that he didn't consider that somewhere out there some bucks around a council fire were hatching plans to make a raid on the whites in the east.

One midday, Paco and Slocum squatted on top of a mound. Their mounts were busy chomping grass through the bits in their mouth. The herd spread out over acres.

"We've close to a thousand head by my tally," said Slocum. "That's plenty of cattle for us to move and winter. We'll need some more supplies. I'd like two good wagons to haul all of our things—we are all scattered out with oxcarts and the things we move with. All we need is a few travois and we'd look like Injuns."

"How much we owe Goeserman?" Paco asked.

"Five hundred."

"How much more money must we have to get there?"

"A thousand dollars, I figure, to get us up there."

Paco narrowed his good eye to look at him. "Whew, can we find that much *cred-it*?"

"We have the cattle. Big steers. We've cut out all the cows."

"*Sí,* what will become of them? The cows that are branded?"

Slocum shifted his weight to the other leg. "I figured you could come back and build a ranch around here and they'd start your herd."

"They would be half yours."

Slocum shook his head and then looked at the dirt. "No, I have ridges to ride over. Places to see. I can't set any roots."

"I am a simple man, but even I can count this many steers are worth something in Missouri. Lots of money."

"Mary will need some to start over too."

"*Sí,* and the vaqueros will need work later too."

"You'll need a registered brand of your own."

"It will be a star—estrella."

"That's up to the brand registry. It may be taken."

Paco nodded. "I let you worry about the business part."

"Hire yourself a young bookkeeper. They don't cost much more than cowhands."

"Really—how can I hire him? I have no money." Paco turned up his calloused brown palms and shook his head.

"We can find one in Fort Worth."

"But the money?"

"Let me worry about that. I need to scout us a route north tomorrow. We need to move on to winter quarters up at Mason like the colonel planned."

"Sometimes, *mi amigo,* I wonder if this is really happening. I am the son of a peon. My father worked hard day and night for a *patrón* on a large hacienda. One day my father died and they turned my mother and my brothers and sisters out. We had to move and live like lizards in the desert."

Slocum smiled at him. "You have not done half bad. He would be proud of you. Estrella Hacienda, that would be nice."

"I told my wife Camille in Mexico when I saw her last that God had sent you to me."

Slocum shook his head. "No, he sent us to be together. I'll scout ahead. Tell Mary I may not be back until tomorrow."

"God be with you, amigo." Paco clapped him on the shoulder and looked very seriously at him from his good eye. No more words were necessary.

After he and Paco parted, Slocum rode his buckskin Pacer north on his search for their way to Mason. He soon moved into a land of dead black mesquite trees. Snags that marked the country before him stood like head markers in a cemetery. Once a forest of trees had dotted the land, but drought had killed them and in the dry air they'd stood for years, maybe centuries, since they'd died. They lent an eerie look to the landscape, along with expansive beds of prickly pear with many dead pads on the shriveled plants.

The portion of lower Texas where they caught the cattle was desolate enough, but this land looked like a place for the dead. He had hoped to find some water, but nothing looked promising. Simply riding across this land for hours had depressed him—the lack of stock water complicated his plans. A two-day drive to water looked like the next option, if he could even find a source that close by. Such a push would be hell on the people and livestock as well.

Then a spot of green in the distance lightened his thoughts. He set Pacer into his high-stepping gait, and soon the view of the thin line of cottonwoods eased his mind some. They meant water. Reining the buckskin up, he noticed signs of a small Indian village along the watercourse. Damn, he'd have to detour around this place—go further away from them or have problems. What tribe were they?

Where were their horses? Why no smoke? He reined Pacer toward the west for some higher ground and a better vantage point. Something was wrong. He couldn't hear any dogs barking either. Maybe the camp had been abandoned?

Pacer lunged going up the steep slope and Slocum reined him up on the crest. He stood in the stirrups to look things over with a critical eye. A narrow stream of brown water snaked through the sandbars under the bluff nurturing the wind-rustled cottonwoods. Several large gnarled trunks, peeled bare in death, marked the course, and the wind fluttered white and red rags hanging on things about the camp. A dozen buffalo-hide lodges were scattered below him on the flat, but nothing stirred. Had all the inhabitants died?

He drew the Colt from his holster. In the high sun's glare, he cocked the hammer and spun the cylinder. The five primer caps were on each nipple. The cylinder under the hammer was not loaded for safety. There was still lard plugging each .44 chamber. That prevented a cross fire or an explosion when shooting the weapon. Satisfied, he slapped the pistol back on his hip and reset the holster. Nothing moved and the only sound was the strong wind rustling the dollar-sized cottonwood leaves.

He leaned back in the saddle as Pacer descended the slope. As he swayed back and forth going downhill, a hard knot began to form in the pit of his stomach. He switched reins and dried his palm on his pants. Still no sound. No dogs. No children. No sign of life. The village had been abandoned. But why? Indians seldom left their hides behind when they left. They'd be too hard to replace.

Pacer stepped high going through the shallow water, and Slocum kept him from drinking by holding his head up. There would be time for that later. First, he had to be certain this was not a trap.

Many articles were strewn about as if left in haste, things Indians did not abandon. An iron pot hung over a dead fire. No squaw would have left without it. A bundle of arrows, a buffalo-hide shield, all things warriors took to their graves or places of final rest. He dismounted and tied Pacer to a bush. The barefoot pony tracks were days old. Even a blackened deer carcass hung rotting from a tree limb too high for coyotes to feed upon it.

A crow called in the distance. He halted and his hand sought his gun butt. He listened till his ears hurt, then walked with caution toward the first lodge. The frame was made of willow hauled there, for he saw none suitable for such construction in this creek bottom. Laced crosswise with rawhide, the hides on the first lodge were still green. When he went to pull the flap back, swarms of green flies went aloft. He removed his hat and looked inside the dark interior. The strong smell of sweat, body musk, and tobacco filled his nose. There were several jugs and even bedding inside. Not things women left behind unless they expected to come back or had to flee an enemy.

He straightened and asked himself, *What drove them away?* Other Indians? The army? Texas Rangers? He backed away from the buzzing flies he'd disturbed. They followed him like bees, as if angry that he had nothing to eat. Soon, the wind drove them away and the crows called again.

What else could he hear? The whimper of a small dog? He listened again, but it was gone. Something small was crying? Maybe a coyote pup. He'd heard them before. No, not that sound. He went from door opening to door opening. Nothing, but he saw the same thing in each dark lodge he stuck his head inside—many personal items had been abandoned in the inhabitants' haste to leave.

Then he stopped and squatted in front of a doorway. The small whine came from this lodge. He carefully checked around outside—the bluff area and the rest of the camp. Pacer stood disinterested, his head down and right hind hoof up in hip-shot fashion. A horse sensed things around him before most dogs even caught wind of it.

There that cry was again. He set his hat down, and with his hand he moved the hide door aside, then stuck his head inside the tent. At the sight of a bare white leg and foot, he drew his gun. Trying to see in the lodge was near impossible. Satisfied the person was probably dead, he backed out and ripped the thick hide back further so sunlight shone in.

The body was that of a naked white woman. The insides of her legs were smeared in black dried blood and her swollen breasts looked blue. Not a girl, but a woman of thirty or so. Her teeth were bared and lips drawn back as if she'd died in pain with her hair crudely chopped short—not a pretty sight. Her wide blue eyes looked at nothing. He felt sick enough to vomit at the sight of her, and had started to duck out when he heard the cry again.

It was a tiny baby lying wrapped in a blanket beside her. Gingerly, he picked it up in his shaky hands. *How long since you last ate, little fellow?* Holy cow, a baby alive in a dead village. And he stank bad. Real bad. What next?

Nothing Slocum could do for the mother. He was hours away from his own camp. Straightening, he went outside with the small package in the crook of his arm and looked him over. The baby sure needed to be cleaned up. It was a wonder the flies had not eaten him alive. At the stream, he did a clumsy job of cleaning the baby, and found another blanket rag to wrap him in.

All this little fella had to do was hang on. The women back in camp would find him something to eat. *You made it this far. Hang tight, little one, we're going to where they've got airtight milk cans.* With a last look around, the bundle in the crook of his arm, he mounted up and set Pacer for his camp. Grateful for the high-stepping horse's ground-gaining pace, he checked the sun time. They needed to hurry.

The baby's weak cries and coughing niggled at him. The miles proved long. What if it died from hunger going back? Should he have fed it something? What? Some rock-hard jerky from his saddlebags? His stomach had the jitters and he urged Pacer on faster—they had a little boy to save.

All he could do was soak the tail of his kerchief in his canteen water and let the baby suck on it. Then resoak it to let the baby ease some more down his dry throat. The best part to Slocum was when the little fellow coughed. Then he would throw him on his shoulder and pat him on the back. He was still alive—thank God.

"Hey! Hey!" he shouted, riding into the cow camp in the twilight. "Mary, Matilda, get out here."

"What's wrong?" Mary asked, holding her skirt up as she ran from the girls' tent.

"I found a baby," he said, stepping down and handing her the small bundle. "He ain't had a thing to eat in days. Can we save him?"

She took the bundle and looked carefully at the small infant in her arms.

"We can try."

"Good," he said, and let his stiff shoulders slump. What a ride.

Mary rushed off with the other women behind her.

"Whose is it? How did you find it?" A million questions came from the vaqueros crowded around Slocum, and they followed on his heels. Tomas took Pacer by the reins, and Slocum instructed him to walk the horse till he cooled.

"Now let me drink a cup of coffee and we can all sit down. Then I'll tell you about one of the strangest things ever happened to me." He bent over and poured himself a cupful. Standing, he motioned to where they all sat on the ground for meals.

"About noon today, I rode up on a dozen lodges." He shook his head and sipped some coffee. "Damnedest thing I ever saw . . ."

14

In late evening, a week later in their new location on Fly Creek, he rode into camp and asked Mary how the little fella had done that day. Airtight milk was bringing him around, but it had been touch-and-go for several days.

"He's going to make it," Mary said with the baby in her arms. "I was worried those first few days, but I think he's going to be fine."

"Good. He's going to have Heck's name if he lives. He could do worse being half Indian and half white," Slocum said.

"He could do lots worse. Heck was a good man."

He agreed. "Guess it's all right here in camp. Everything going smooth?"

"Sure, why?"

"In the morning I'm going to ride up to Mason and try to find where the colonel was going to winter there."

"How far away is that?"

"Maybe a hundred miles. Take me a week anyway to get up there, find out what I need to know, and get back to the herd. But we need to know where we can graze them till the grass breaks in the spring."

She looked at him concerned. "Lots of cattle."

"Lots and they'd eat lots of grass too. But Paco and the boys have this cattle driving down good. They'll be fine. You girls keep an eye out. We're still in Comanche country all the way up to Fort Worth." He bent over and used his finger to flick the blanket back to see little Heck's wrinkled tan face and small fists.

"Heck, keep fighting," he said.

She dropped her voice. "Rosa is caring for him tonight. Leave room in the blankets for me."

He tipped his hat to her. "I shall. I better go eat before Matilda throws it out."

"Oh, she'd never do that. You're her favorite cowboy."

"I need to be someone's favorite." He placed both hands on his hips and strained his sore back as he headed for the cooking fire. Damn, he was sure stiff from all this cattle driving.

Before daylight the next morning, he sat up in the bedroll they'd shared, leaned over, and kissed her. "I hear pots banging."

"Oh, well, I better go help. You ride easy going up there. We all have a stake in you." She began to dress, putting on her blouse. "You know that."

He hugged her. This entire business had been some kind of a dream. Finding Mary, Paco for a partner. He'd have to thank the colonel if he ever saw him in the hereafter for making it all possible. They were still a long way from Sedalia, and they had many things to cross through that would never be easy, but the cowboys were doing their part. Concerned about having enough riding stock in the cavvy, Paco wanted more horses rounded up and broke before spring and the final drive. Plus Slocum would need to gather more supplies on credit. Wary of the days ahead before he even started out, he shook his head in the predawn coolness, seated on the bedding and pulling on his boots. Just another morning . . .

After a long hot day in the saddle, he found a water source and threw down his bedroll. Then he hobbled Roan to graze, and gnawed on some beef jerky for his supper while the coyotes sang him a lullaby. He figured he was a third of the way there. Two more days riding he'd be in the frontier town of Mason and maybe find the colonel's pasturage.

The next day, he saw the Texas flag flying over a low set of building and corrals. Some frontier trading post, no doubt, and he reined Roan in the direction of the place set under a few spindly cottonwoods and with a hand-dug well.

The sign said, BRISTOW'S TRADN POST. Four hip-shot horses stood at the hitch rack. Dried salt on their shoulders told him they'd been rode hard and put away wet. Two wore Texas saddles and the other two McClellan army rigs. That was not his concern. However, they could be outlaws or just renegades on the prowl. The latter meant they were looking for trouble with whoever they could find and wherever they could find it. Guns, knives, or fists, it made no difference to them. Their kind would rather fight than eat. As if they lacked something in their lives when they weren't seeking or involved in some kind of scuffle. Hard men who came out of the war bitter—ruthless, like they wanted to hurt everyone in their path,

When Slocum stepped down, he felt leery about finding such a set of men inside the low-roofed post. Must have been hundreds like them—the damn war brought it all on. Maybe they felt cheated when they came home alive and all their pards were buried in some cotton field in the South. No way to run from them, no place to go. Slocum'd mind his own business as long as they'd let him.

He adjusted the .44 and took off his hat to wipe his wet forehead on his sleeve, then reset it. His eyes squinted against the midday glare reflecting off the hot ground as he strode for the open door. Actually, there was no door on the hand-hewn board frame. In cold weather, they must have tacked a blanket or hide over it for closure.

Forced to duck going in, he let his vision adjust to the candlelit darkness. First, a few figures emerged in sight as he straightened. A short Mexican woman in a low-cut blouse came swishing her way over suggestively to greet him. A man behind a full dark mustache and polishing a glass nodded to him from behind the bar. The four men playing cards acted too engrossed in their card game to look aside—but they stole glances to measure him.

One wore a felt hat with a gold-braid band two of them

wore gray forage caps, and the fourth one a big sombrero.

"Welcome to Fort McKay," the woman said and stepped in close in a familiar way. "You are lonesome, no?"

"No, not right now," Slocum said in a low voice. "Maybe later."

With her shoulders back, she pushed her ample breasts toward him and smiled. "My name is Lolita."

He touched his hat. "Nice to meet you, Lolita."

Then she held out her brown hand toward the bar. "Carlos will pour you something."

"I could use a drink." He nodded and smiled at her.

A chair scraped and the one in the sombrero stood up. "I think that's plumb insulting to the little lady there."

His words drew a titter of laughter from the cardplayers as they cut looks around at Slocum. He paused about halfway to the bar and turned back to look at the big man, who was now standing. With a slow nod of consideration, Slocum used his thumb to push his hat back and look over the huskily built challenger. With a pained expression on his face, Slocum asked, "Did I miss your name?"

"Williams—Colonel Iram Williams."

"Slocum's mine. I came in here for a drink and I'll be riding on, I trust. I really don't have time to notify your next of kin."

No mistaking the menacing look on the colonel's face that Slocum's words had drawn out of him.

"You saying—"

"Colonel—" The boy wearing a cap on the colonel's right jumped up and interceded. "I know him. He was a captain in the Georgia Thirty-second."

Williams folded his arm over his chest as if appraising Slocum. "He don't look like officer material to me."

"He was, sir. I knowed him from Tennessee." The youth's wide eyes darted to the others at the table. "He was a hero there."

"Hero, huh?"

"Yes, sir. Battle of Goose Crick, sir."

"Hmm." Williams snorted out his nose. "Billy Jack here says you're a hero."

"I was there," Slocum said, slumped a little in his stance and turned more sideways to face the man so he presented a minimal target when or if the shooting ever started.

Williams rubbed his palms on the sides of his pants legs. A slight smile crossed his full lips. Like a coiled diamondback with his tail buzzing over his back—ready to strike.

If he thought the look was cunning, he was wrong. Slocum felt they were at the brink. Either Williams pressed on or he eased off. His call. Slocum aimed to finish it. Besides, he was thirsty. Then a flicker in the man's hard brown eyes betrayed him. The muscles in Slocum's arm readied for action. The fingers on his right hand were in an open clawlike position to jerk the .44 clear of the holster, cock, and fire it. Milliseconds passed, both men frozen in readiness.

A small tick in the muscle on the right side of Slocum's jaw began to pulsate like a trip hammer. *Go for it, you sumbitch. It's a good day to die.* His eyes, dry from the wind, glare, and heat, became steady and hard focused on the big man's slightest shift.

Then, as if he considered the whole thing a mistake, Williams raised his hands and waved Slocum off. "No need in two brothers of the South having a misunderstanding, is there?"

"Your choice."

"Well, join us. Boys here and I are having a friendly game of poker."

"Thanks. I'll have me a drink at the bar and ride on."

"Hmm, must be pretty pressing business to cause you to be on the move like that."

Slocum nodded and turned to walk to the bar.

"We could always use another man—"

He shook his head, put his left arm on the bar, and nodded to the stone-faced man behind the bar. Without turning, he said over his shoulder. "Thanks, I've got work."

Slocum could see Williams's image in the smoky mirror

behind the bar. He made a face at Slocum's back and then sat down.

"Ah, Señor," the woman said, and rushed in to hug his waist. Looking up with an eager smile and her breasts shoved into his side, she said, "Why rush away? We could go to my place and have a party."

"Darling, I'd love to but I have business to attend to." He nodded at the bartender's choice of whiskey, and the man brought the bottle and glass to him.

"Business, business." She stepped in and ran her palm familiarly over his fly. "You and I could do much business in my bed."

He poured himself some liquor in a glass. Still on edge and not satisfied that Williams might not try something before he was through, he tossed down the whiskey. It cut the dust on his tongue and burned a path down his throat. He felt it slide clear to his stomach, and it even warmed his ears. With a nod of approval at the bartender, he poured two more fingers in the glass.

Attached to him like a tick, she wasn't going to give up. Her fingers groped and played with him until he gently took her shoulder and pressed her a little ways aside. With a wink at her, he ordered another glass for her and poured two fingers in it.

He raised his and clinked it to hers. "To another day."

Making a disappointed face, she nodded, then smiled again. "I can't wait."

When his second drink was down, he paid the man six bits. With her hugging his waist possessively, he headed for the bright doorway. She let go at the opening, and he stopped to let his eyes focus on the brilliance outside.

"Have a nice day, gents," he said to the cardplayers over his shoulder, and went for Roan.

If they did more than grunt, he never heard them.

In the saddle, he looked back at the saloon one last time—somewhere, sometime, his and Williams's paths would cross again. The next time might not end as smoothly. He reined Roan to the north. He had winter grazing to find.

15

Mason was a small frontier town hugging the edge of Comanche territory with its backside against the hill country and facing the flatter desert country to the west. It had been settled mostly by Germans, and the Lutheran church's spire stood above the live oak trees. Slocum stopped at the public watering trough and watered Roan. While he was busy undoing the girth, he eyed the row of saloons and businesses. Where would he start looking for someone who knew anything about Colonel Banks's plans to winter a herd around there?

When Roan was through drinking his fill, Slocum led him across the dusty street to the rack in front of Marcham's Saloon. The black letters were painted on the plank-board false front. He hitched Roan, went through the swinging doors, and stood in the sour-smelling, dark room, letting his eyes adjust.

"Velcome to Mason!" a man with a thick black beard shouted from behind the bar.

Three men playing cards at a side table hardly paid him any interest. He ventured over and studied the large mirror on the back bar. Much larger than most. He nodded to the man.

"Vat you want?" the man asked.

"A cold beer?"

"I got cool beer. No ice in dis country."

"Draw me a cool one then." Slocum smiled at the big man.

"You are passing through?"

"I'm really seeking some information. A man named Colonel Banks planned on using some grazing land around here this fall and winter."

The man shrugged and delivered the mug overflowing with foam. "Could be. Dere is lots of grazing west of town. Open range, huh?"

"You never heard of a Colonel Banks?"

"No, my name is Marcham." He offered his hand and they pressed the flesh over the bar.

"Slocum's mine. I guess the colonel came through here, saw that range, and decided it would be a good place to winter." When his host nodded, Slocum raised the mug and sipped the cool beer. Not cold, but at least evaporatively cooled. He nodded his approval and dug out a dime to pay.

A short man rose from the card game and came over. "My name's Smith. I know the colonel. Where is he?"

"Well, Mr. Smith, that's a mystery too. His crew was murdered and we were unable to find his body at the scene."

"Smith's good enough, I ain't no mister."

"Where did you know the colonel from?"

"War. I served under him."

Slocum nodded and raised the mug for another sip. "When did you see him last?"

"About nine months ago here. He was trying to buy a bunch of neck yokes."

"Did he lease any outfit for his winter headquarters around here you know about?"

Smith shook his head. "Told me he was going to use the old Bar C."

"No one live there now?"

"Pack rats and jackrabbits."

Slocum set down his beer and wiped his mouth on his sleeve. "What happened to the Bar C?"

"What gets all them folks that try to go too far out there—Comanches got them."

"Is there water out there?"

"You don't sound any smarter than Banks did."

Slocum hoisted the glass for another drink. This sawed-off puncher sounded like he knew enough to get him there. "I'm probably not. Can you show me the place?"

"When?"

"This afternoon?"

"It'll take some time to get out there. A half-day ride out there. I don't know, it may be all burned down by now."

"I'd like to see it. I'd pay you to take me out there."

Smith nodded and hitched up his pants. "I could sure use a beer."

"Mr. Marcham, draw my friend a cool one."

"Coming up."

Slocum put his elbows on the bar and studied his own dust-floured personage in the mirror back of the bar. Not very impressive-looking for a man who needed a couple thousand bucks worth of credit for food and supplies until spring broke nine months from then. No need in going much farther if he couldn't find any.

"Who's the biggest merchant in town?" he asked the two.

"Goldman," Marcham said, and Smith nodded.

"I need some supplies for this drive. He worth talking to?"

"Charges a hundred percent interest."

"I could stand that."

"What've you got for collateral?" Smith asked, using a kerchief to wipe his mustache dry from the foam off his beer.

"A thousand steers and seventy horses."

"He might talk to you." Smith looked at the barman with a questioning look.

Marcham frowned his thick black eyebrows. "Vere you going to sell them?"

"Sedalia, Missouri."

"No more. They got all the roads barred up there. They say the longhorns got tick fever and it kills their cattle."

"Well, someone needs them." Slocum looked at both of them. He'd find a market.

Marcham shook his head in surrender, like he didn't believe there was any use in talking anymore. "They gawdamn sure ain't worth much down here. You can go talk to Goldman."

"Reckon I can. Where will I meet you in the morning?" he asked Smith.

"Here. I'll be ready whenever."

"Sunup. I'll be out in front."

"I'll have my horse and kit. You getting us a few things to eat?"

"I'll handle it."

"Ain't no damn cafés out there."

Slocum paid for the beers and nodded. Best he went and found Goldman next. Wondering what sort of a man the merchant was, he stepped out in the afternoon glare and squinted against it. Across the street, the faded letters were on the adobe wall: GOLDMAN MERC. The rest of the letters were gone. Folks no doubt knew what the large building contained—no need in wasting money on another sign.

The store smelled of raw wool—a smell of sheep that penetrated his sinuses with a strong whang when he stepped inside the doorway. A sheep bell rang overhead, and a pair of sharp dark eyes cut through the store's shadowy interior piled high with merchandise on tables, a mountain of one-size-fits-all shoes, sandals, straw hats, overalls, bolts of material, blankets, scrapes, ponchos, rolls of leather cowhides, hardware, and tools.

"What's your pleasure, mister?" the man asked with a ring of impatience in his tone. Bent over some figures he worked on, he barely gave Slocum a glance.

"The name Colonel Banks mean anything to you?"

He indicated no, and some of the black hair fell over his forehead. "Should it?"

"He said he planned to winter a large herd of cattle around here."

The man shook his head as if he'd had enough of their

conversation, and went back to his calculation on the butcher paper atop the counter with a pencil. "Plenty of land around here. He could do it anywhere."

"No, the colonel was going to do it around here at Mason."

"Where is this colonel now?" The man looked up hard at Slocum.

"I don't know. Some no-good outlaws shot his camp up and killed all his men. We couldn't find his body."

"What's all that got to do with me?"

"I need a stake for enough grub to get my crew through till spring."

"I ain't charity."

"I've got a thousand steers."

The man looked up at him and then used his forearm to straighten upright. "Well, they're about as valuable as lily pads are around here."

"I'm taking them to Sedalia and the railhead in the spring."

"What're they worth there?"

"Ten cents a pound."

"That makes an eight-hundred-pound steer worth eighty dollars."

Slocum nodded.

"And how do I know you'll ever come back and pay me?"

Slocum shook his head slowly and picked up a new jack-knife off the counter to examine it. "Mister, ain't nothing certain but death. However, if I don't get killed, I'll be back in the fall to pay you."

"I charge a hundred percent interest. A barrel of flour costs you twenty dollars—cash ten."

With a nod to show that he'd heard the man, he set the knife back down. "I savvy. Do we have a deal?"

"Most men would scream at those prices."

"I'm a realist and I'll pay you."

"So you are. When'll your herd be coming in here?" He backed up and parked his butt on the low counter behind him. "Say your name once more."

"Slocum. They'll be up here in a week or so."

"Slocum, my name's Estes Goldman."

Slocum stuck out his hand and they shook.

"I've got a paper here you might want to read." Goldman reached under the counter and brought out a printed page. "Fella came by here a few days ago talking about a new market. Out in Kansas."

"Where?"

"You ever heard of Abilene?"

"No, sir." Slocum looked at the signature on the bottom. *Joe McCoy*. Who in the hell was he?

"New shipping point. Past the damn farmers. It might be for real. This fella came in by here and talked my leg off about it last week. I says, who's dumb enough to go up there with cattle?"

"His reply?"

"Anyone that likes the color of money."

"This McCoy was here?" Slocum asked, thumping his fingers on the name.

"No, he said McCoy was building pens up there this winter."

"What did you think?"

Goldman raised both eyebrows and nodded. "I believe I'd head for there if I had any cattle to sell. Them stories about Bald Knobbers and guerrillas in Arkansas and Missouri don't sound good."

"You get me enough grub to feed this outfit to get us up there, and I'll pay your twenty dollars a barrel."

Goldman stuck out his hand and they shook on it. "Slocum, where're you going next?"

"Bar C in the morning. Some cowboy's showing me the way out there. I need a place to hold them till spring."

"A man ain't got any more sense than drive cattle due north would go there."

"You got a better place to winter a thousand head?"

"No. But it's too close to the Comanches for me."

"We'll see."

"Does any bank own them cattle?"

"Nope, not now. Paco and I do."

"Guess I'll meet this Paco in time."

Slocum nodded. "You will, and I get set up, I'll be after that high-priced grub."

Goldman nodded his head slowly as if considering the matter. "If you got any hair left, you will."

Slocum left the store with some jerky, dried cheese, and crackers in a poke to take on the trip out to the Bar C. He wondered about the Indian threat. Must be serious. Still, he needed the place to winter—going very far north this time of year would only lead to disaster. When the new grass appeared in the spring, then he'd—The words on the bill said take the wagon tracks north from the Red River to Jesse Chisholm's trading post at Council Oaks, then use Jesse's Road to the Salt Fork of the Arkansas, and from that point follow the new furrow and piles of sod to Abilene. The trail was well marked, the bill said.

It better be. It sure better be.

16

The next morning Slocum met Smith and learned he was
called Shorty. He had a wide-brim hat, a neck rag of gray
silk, batwing chaps, a vest to pocket his tobacco makings in,
a longhorn mustache all twisted at the ends. He was too
bowlegged to hire to herd hogs. They'd all escape running
under him. Slocum bought them each some hot tamales
from a Mexican woman in the street.

Her coffee was a shade bitter, but Slocum had a notion
that when he got back from this trip it might be flavorful.
After Slocum paid her, Shorty mounted a bay horse that
snorted wearily in the dust. With his saddle and lariat tied
on, he looked real enough. Time would tell the rest. They
set out west through the low greasewood and mesquite.
There was some dried bunchgrass, and Slocum figured
those old brush-eaters would find enough to exist on till
spring.

Close to noon, Slocum heard something that sounded like
bells, and indicated by hand signal for Shorty to head into
the cover of the dry wash.

"What's wrong?"

"We've got us company," Slocum hissed at his protest. He
couldn't see anything, but he'd heard the bell. It might be a
sheep bell, but he wanted to take no chances. In the wash, he

dismounted and gave the pale-faced Shorty the reins to his horse.

"Keep them quiet. I'm going to sneak a peek and try to see who's out there."

Shorty's Adam's apple bobbed hard. "Yes, sir."

Slocum removed his hat and climbed to the top of the wash. From there he could make out four bucks—rusty red-colored skin, their braided hair the same color from the dirt, filthy eagle feathers flopping in the rising wind. They were wearing loincloths of leather and moccasins heels that beat a tattoo on their animals' ribs. They led two white captives on horses. One of the bucks beat the lagging horses with his quirt to make them jog. That was the source of the ringing.

Another buck carried a rifle. The other two were armed with bows and arrows. At a medium range they could sink an arrowhead into someone's heart. In fact, most Indians were more dangerous with bows and arrows than firearms.

The white bone vest of one Indian looked like it was made from polished ivory, with bright brass beads on it for decoration. They were not boys, but hard-faced men. The two children's tears had streaked their dirty faces, but the boy and girl were long past crying.

"Holy Jesus," Shorty said in a whisper from beside him.

"Get back to them horses. They whinny one time, we're dead meat."

"Yes, sir." Shorty fled.

Dumb sumbitch anyway. He could get them both killed. Slocum's eyes were still focused on the Indian lashing the horses. Over the rising wind he could still hear his bells. Tiny silver ones.

What could he do about the captives? Nothing much. Shorty wouldn't be any help. If Paco was there, they could take on the four of them. But his one-eyed partner was miles south with the herd. If Slocum managed to get the children away from them and any of the bucks escaped him, they'd bring back a pack of savages to kill him. Yet—he still needed to do something.

What? Good question. Send Shorty after help? Slocum

couldn't imagine him raising a tough posse out of those German farmers he'd seen on the street in Mason. Ill-armed and inadequate would sum up their fighting ability even against only four warriors.

When the Comanche went over the next rise, he slipped back in the dry wash. When he spotted Shorty by the horses, the man was pissing a full stream out of a dick that would have made a donkey proud.

"Damn, are they gone?" He looked to be uncontrollably shaken by the encounter.

"For now."

"For now?" His voice was shrill and his blue eyes blinked in disbelief.

"Hush. They've got two children as hostages."

"Well-well-what the shit can we do—do about that."

"Try to get them back."

"Holy sweet Jesus. You—you're crazy. Nuts. They'll kill us too."

"Those are children out there."

"No—no—they ain't got a chance anyway, so why we going to get killed?" He swallowed hard.

"'Cause we ain't savages. You got a gun?"

"Sure, but I ain't—"

"Get it out and be sure it's loaded. I have a .44, this Spencer, and a .30-caliber five-shot pistol in my saddlebags."

Shorty fumbled in his things. "I ain't no damn pistolero."

At last, Shorty produced a handgun. He handed it to Slocum and then took a wild look around.

"I thought you were in the army," Slocum said. He looked at the rusty weapon Shorty had handed him. "This thing hasn't been fired—"

"Been years since I found it."

"I can see that. We better disassemble it and start over. It's .44 caliber. My ammo will fit it."

"I got over killing folks and me being in the line of fire in the war. I ain't going no Comanche hunting with you. Captives or no captives."

"Well, you can run back to town. They might not catch you." '

"Catch me? Why? Why?"

"Just shut up," Slocum said. "You can take this pistol and ride with me and try to help me. Or you can run off."

"Help you?" Shorty's voice became shriller.

"Help me. Now settle down. We have four firearms. They have one."

"Bow, arrows, axes, knives. Shit fire, they cut folks' nuts off alive and eat them raw in their faces."

"They ever do that to you?" Slocum went for his extractor. He needed to unload the weapon, clean it best he could, and reload it for the obviously shaken cowboy.

"Nooo—and once more, they ain't getting the chance to do that to me."

"Well, I can clean and reload this pistol and then we can go see how tough they really are. Or you can run back to town and cry like a baby. What'll it be?"

"You figure there may be more of them, don't you? More between here and town?"

"I figure usually they have several small bands out capturing children, and they'll be joining back up at some camp later."

Shorty nodded like he had all the information under his hat. "I fought in Mississippi. I never knew why. I hated that skeeter country. I hated cotton. I fought them bluebellies for acres of it. In the end we lost. I came home barefooted, busted down. For six months I couldn't even get up a hard-on."

"That's bad. But them two kids deserve our help."

"Worse'n bad. I was just coming back from all that. I mean, I could finally sleep at night—now."

"What if you were that boy? Wouldn't you want someone to save you?"

"Hell, yes, but I ain't no hero. I wasn't a hero in the war and I ain't improved none since then. You can fix that pistol—but—but I ain't no hand with shooting one."

Slocum drew out the first ball with the T-shaped screw.

Only three cylinders were loaded. When it had been fired last, he wasn't sure. "Take off your hat and go look around. Be sure they ain't coming back."

"Oh, dear God—" Shorty moaned, but he obeyed.

The cylinder was soon cleared and the firing holes under the nipples were cleared. Slocum felt the gun should fire for Shorty—if he could use it. Many enlisted men had never shot a pistol in the war or in their lives. Maybe they had had a shotgun at home, or even a .22. Shorty acted like a man with not much firing experience. Time would tell. This boy wasn't the picture of bravery that Slocum would have liked to have—but Shorty was all that was available.

Slocum worked some lard over the rusty parts to make the gun operate smoother, then reloaded five cylinders and rested the hammer on the empty one. At this point, all he could do was pray they caught the four Indians off guard before they reached the main party.

He joined Shorty on the rim. "See anything of them?"

"No."

"Stick it in your belt." He handed him the revolver. "It's loaded."

Gingerly, Shorty took the weapon and stuck it behind his waistband. "I hope you know what you're doing. I sure don't."

"I do."

"Good, 'cause I'm about ready to puke over this deal."

"We both may do that then. Let's get our horses."

17

They were bellied down and creeping toward the campfire that made an orange glow in the starlit sea of greasewood. Slocum led the way. Both of them were slithering like snakes to get close enough to surprise the camp. Pausing to take the stickers out of their hands at intervals, they inched toward their goal—the Comanche war party.

Dancing, stomping, and chanting, the Comanches sounded loud in the night. The bells rang clear when the wearer joined in the celebration. Comanches were not the most ceremonial people, not usually holding special dances like other tribes did. This was a man's society. They respected only the virile, the buffalo hunter, the killer of his enemies, the mighty male. A male who didn't measure up would be killed or commit suicide. Women were lowly servants and provided labor and children. A woman had to keep herself ugly and unkempt so no other man but her husband would desire her. She risked the loss of her nose if she didn't obey. If her husband suspected she was having an affair with someone else, he would cut the tendons on her heels so she had to crawl about doing her work and tending her children.

Even mountain men ignored the unbathed Comanche women. One old man that Slocum had met in Saint Louis after the war called them all "rotten crotches." Said they smelled worse than a dead cow. All his years on the frontier, he said, he always avoided the Comanches' filthy camps and stinking females. It was the only pussy the old man said he ever passed up, and by his own admission he'd screwed some sorry ones in his day.

Using his elbows to propel him, Slocum advanced inches closer at a time. The tempo of the Indians' hell-raising grew louder and faster. The drumbeat thumped like a bad headache in both of Slocum's ears. When he glanced back, he could see Shorty coming after him. Good—despite all his fears, the cowboy was along for backup—good shot or not. Sometimes just having bullets flying helped. Slocum hoped his plan to surprise the Comanches worked.

Then he dried his sweaty right hand on the side of his leg, and paused for a moment. In the fire's light he could make out the bloodred figure as he ripped off his loincloth and held the protruding erection in his hand. Scooting forward flat-footed as if advancing on some target with his long spear, he threw his head back and howled loud enough to cause the skin on the sides of Slocum's face to draw up.

The captive girl's scream filled the night. Those others must be holding her down for him, Slocum decided, since he could hear her struggling. *Damn them.*

"Now!" Slocum hissed, and was on his feet aiming down the rifle's sight on the move. The rifle blasted an orange muzzle flash. The naked Indian staggered forward a few steps, then fell. Another rose up and Slocum took aim. He squeezed off the trigger and his bullet spun the screaming brave halfway around.

"Get that other one!" he shouted at Shorty.

The revolver bucked in Shorty's hand as he shot at the third Indian, then rushed forward in pursuit of the last buck, who was fleeing the camp. Straddling bushes and jumping others, Shorty was hot on his trail. He fired all five shots before he drew to a halt.

Good, he got the fourth one. Slocum went to the girl's side and knelt beside her, noting both bucks he had shot were on the ground and not moving. He dropped on his haunches beside her.

"You all right?"

Numbly, she nodded, sitting up and frantically pushing her tattered dress tail over her bare legs.

"Where's the boy?"

She gave a nod toward the shadows, and Slocum saw the bound youth seated on his butt between two bushes. Slocum glanced in Shorty's direction and shouted, "You get both of them?"

"Ya. . . ."

"You okay?"

"Hmmhmm."

"What's your name?" Slocum asked the girl. He'd have time for Shorty later.

"Darla."

"Slocum's my name. I better untie the boy."

She nodded, still in shock. Slocum patted her shoulder and moved to the boy. "How are you?"

"Pretty scared," he said in a small voice.

With his jackknife, Slocum cut the leather ties on his wrist and feet. "You all right now?"

"I think—think so—" He rubbed his sore wrists.

"Good. What's your name?"

"Hertz."

"Hertz, you see about Darla. She's upset and we understand. Right?"

He nodded. "I was sure scared for her."

"So was I. But she's fine. I better check on Shorty." He pushed off his knees and rose to his feet. Where was his man?

Then he saw the silhouette of his hat and strode over there. "You all right?"

"S-sure—just kinda sick to my stomach."

"I understand."

"No, I went though the whole damn war. I don't think I ever shot a man. Oh, I shot, but I never knew if I hit anyone. I pissed all over myself at Corinth when them bluebellies charged us. Yet when I got up back there I knowed it was me or them. I didn't care about nothing else."

"It ain't never easy."

Obviously shaking, Shorty threw back his shoulders to reinforce himself. "I won't ever be afraid again."

"Afraid?"

"Ya, you know, afraid."

"Good. We better find all their guns and ammo, what things they stole, and get out of here."

"What about their bodies?"

"We'll take them too and cave a dry wash bank over them somewhere else."

Shorty nodded. "We can handle that. Slocum, you reckon you can even winter cattle out here?"

"I'll figure a way."

"I bet you do. What about the kids?"

"We'll take them home."

"Ya. I'd like to go home." Shorty dropped his head as if in defeat.

"Where's that?" Slocum asked.

"Hell, there ain't one. My folks all died with the fever while I was in the war."

"Lots of bad baggage. We've all got some. We better reload that pistol too." Slocum turned on his heel and headed back for the camp.

"Yeah, Slocum. Do you need some help with them cattle? I mean, I'd work for my food."

He paused, looked back at the man. "I might need some."

"Good. I've got a chance then anyway."

Slocum stopped, nodded, and then listened to the coyote's mournful howling for his mate. "Let's clean this up and move out of here."

"Coming."

Sixteen-year-old Hertz Von Louder said he lived near Mason. Fourteen-year-old Darla Rouse's family's place was nearby. Both had been herding their families' sheep bands on Oak Creek when the savages burst in and took them captive. Riding in the rear, Slocum led the two ponies loaded with the four bodies. Something about those two kids wasn't being said. He couldn't put his finger on it. The kids' stories did not sound alike, like they were covering something up. The notion niggled at him as he rode on.

At mid-morning, they buried the four bucks under a dry wash bank they caved in on top of them. It was a relief to have the burden gone. It was a good job, and after much tracking around to confuse any red tracker that might want to investigate, they rode on to the Bar C headquarters.

The place was situated on a shallow brown stream that shifted from sandbar to sandbar. A few gnarled cottonwoods lined the bank. The place was adobe-walled about six feet high around the perimeter. Slocum considered it defensible with repeating rifles. The jacales were in poor repair, but the large pens inside the compound could hold a large cavvy at night.

The desert graze in the area looked like the rest of Texas west of the hill country, sparse dried bunchgrass in the creosote brush, but ample enough to winter on. The colonel had had a good idea planning to use the Bar C for his winter quarters—save for the Comanche. That would be their worst enemy—but a half-dozen repeating rifles in the hands of defenders might be enough to run them off. That and some blasting powder charges set off at intervals might persuade any Indian to leave and stay away.

"What're you thinking now?" Shorty asked, breaking into his thoughts.

"Who owns this place now?"

"Damned if I know. I heard they were all killed by Injuns."

Slocum was watching the two white captives talking to each other in the shade. Still, there was something there untold. He shook his head and turned back to Shorty.

"They ain't told it all to us, have they?" the cowboy asked in a hushed voice.

"Not yet. No idea of the owner's name?"

"No. Wonder what they're hiding from telling us."

"Let's head back for Mason. I expect their folks will be glad to see them."

Shorty nodded, but from his look, Slocum knew he wasn't satisfied.

They rode into the night, leading the kids' horses and two spare ponies while Darla and Hertz rode buffalo ponies. They were drawing close to Mason when Hertz asked Slocum to stop.

Thinking the boy had to piss, he halted the train. The youth pushed his pony in close. "Mr. Slocum. We can't go home."

With a frown, Slocum pushed his hat up and looked hard in the night's dim light for an answer. "Why not?"

"Her father will put her away in a convent."

"Why?"

"Cause she's ah—soiled."

"You think she's soiled?"

"No—no—I love her."

"Then why is he going to think that?"

"'Cause—'cause them Injuns done it to her."

Slocum could hear her sobbing on her horse a few feet away. "He will, he will," she cried.

"Can you support a wife?"

"If I had a job."

"How good are you with figures?"

"I know all my tables. I can make change. I had five years of schooling."

"What are you thinking?" Shorty asked.

"I'm wondering if a judge would marry them when we get to Mason."

"For two bucks, Henry Brower would marry a billy goat. He's the justice of the peace."

"I've got five dollars. Ride in and get him. We'll wait here. We've got to wash the bride's face. You'll find us. Bring the judge." Shorty headed for town in the dark.

Hertz blinked his eyes and hugged Darla, who'd run over to him. "That easy?" he asked Slocum.

"Nothing is going to be easy. But if you two are sure this is the answer, I'll help you."

"Her father told me in no uncertain terms not to herd my

sheep close to hers. I tried to talk to him, but he wouldn't listen and he beat her over it."

Slocum scratched under the too-long hair on his neck. "You ever keep books for a business?"

"No, but I can learn how."

"This outfit needs a bookkeeper."

"Yes, sir. What does it pay?"

"Food and a place for both of you till we get to Abilene."

"Where's that?"

"Kansas. Then you'll get your wages."

"Good."

"You can tell me in Kansas how good it was."

"Will this work?" she asked in a small voice. "Will we really be married?"

"As far as God and the State of Texas are concerned you will be."

"He—he can't beat her anymore?"

"No, Hertz. She'll be yours."

"Oh, I won't ever beat her."

"Better not because I'm going to be your best man here this morning and I ever hear of it, I'll come back and beat *you*."

They laughed.

When the sun was coming up, Shorty returned with a passel of folks driving buggies, carriages, hacks, buckboards, and on horseback and even on mules. They carried flowers and food. Slocum was not too pleased with his entourage, thinking a simple ceremony in the middle of the dusty wagon tracks would be good enough.

"This is Henry," Shorty announced to Slocum, and the man removed a top hat and bowed.

"I understand you wish my services, sir."

"I do. Hertz and Darla wish to be joined in matrimony."

"Oh, my, they are both alive and safe?" He looked at the throng of people surrounding them.

"Get to hitching them," Slocum said.

"Now?"

"Right now." Slocum waved his hand high enough for

Hertz to see it. "Get over here. The wedding is about to proceed."

Women were swooning, carrying their skirts and running in a mob. The men were asking Hertz many questions until the two stopped before the judge.

"Hush!" Slocum shouted, and the judge began his ceremony.

"We are gathered here today—"

"Stop! Stop!" I was a man who'd rushed up in a buggy, waving and shouting. "No!"

"Shorty, go shut him up for the duration of the service." Slocum's frown of impatience even silenced the onlookers' whispering. "Your Honor, proceed."

The cowboy rushed to obey him and confronted the man. After a brief exchange of words, Shorty clubbed him over the head with his pistol. The man went down and silence reigned.

". . . I now pronounce you man and wife. You may kiss the bride."

Everyone cheered. They rushed the young couple with congratulations and a million questions about the kidnapping. A large woman pulled on Slocum's sleeve. "Come, we got breakfast for everyone."

Good, he could use some. "I'm coming."

"You have wife?" she asked.

"Oh, yes," he said as she towed him toward a wagon tailgate laden with food.

She leaned over as if to examine him as they went by, and then straightened. "She don't feed you so good."

They both laughed.

He and Shorty were seated cross-legged on the ground in the shade of a farm wagon. Both of them were nursing their third or fourth beer. It was stout dark beer too. Not pulque.

"Hated I had to bust him over the head, but that Rouse fella wasn't going to shut up."

Slocum clinked his glass mug to Shorty's. "I've got to hand it to you, you damn sure weren't afraid either."

"No, I wasn't, was I?"

18

Hertz and his bride drove a small carriage after them. Shorty led the Indian ponies and Slocum rode Roan in the lead. When they reached the herd, there seemed to be more people there. The women came rushing out drying their hands to greet them.

Mary had a bundle in her arms, so Slocum smiled. Little Heck was still making it.

Paco rode in at a short lope. He reined up hard short of Slocum. "How you do?"

Slocum used his fingers. "Got us a ranch to use. Got us some credit." He held the third finger. "Shorty here's a cowboy. Got a bookkeeper, Hertz, and his wife, Darla, and four more ponies."

Standing in the stirrups and looking over the new horses, Paco scowled. "Did I send you off to kill Comanches?"

Slocum shook his head. "They simply got in the way."

Both men laughed.

Slocum used his tongue to loosen a strand of jerky from breakfast and nodded. "Plus a place we can winter the herd. It isn't heaven, but it has some live water and should keep the cattle in the area without lots of riding herd."

"You learn anything about the colonel up there?"

Slocum shook his head and indicated Shorty. "He talked to him when he was up there. But the colonel only told him he needed ox yokes and was going to use the Bar C, the place we looked at."

Shorty nodded.

Paco shook his head. "You ain't the bookkeeper then."

"Naw, that's Hertz. I'm just the cowboy."

"*Bueno,* we need them too." With a tip of his sombrero to the married pair in the buggy, Paco turned his horse and waved them toward camp.

"What do you really think of this place to spend the winter?" Paco asked Slocum riding stirrup to stirrup with him.

"Good enough. It's no fancy hacienda. With a few more Spencers we can defend it from the Comanche."

"What else you learn up there?"

"We're taking the herd to Abilene, Kansas."

"I thought Missouri."

"New deal. Joe McCoy is the man and he's got a market out on the prairie."

"What about Sedalia?"

"We're going to Abilene."

Paco frowned and shook his head in dismay. "How do you ever get there?"

"Pretty simple," Shorty said. "There's tracks all the way and he's plowed a furrow the last quarter of the way."

"Good, you can be the guide." Paco threw his head back and laughed louder. "Slocum, you are some hombre."

Mary and her baby met them.

"How's he doing?" Slocum asked, dismounting and giving his reins to Tomas.

"He's doing just fine." She showed the sleepy red face, which yawned at him.

"Well, good. How are you?"

"Fine, you find a place?"

"Yes, an old ranch we can stay in till spring."

"Good. I'm worried about this winter."

"It'll be fine. You'll have a roof over your head."

She smiled. "I missed you."

He nodded. He'd missed her too. Parting with her would

not be easy when the time came. That needled him. One day, he'd have to ride on—maybe not . . .

At the meeting around the campfire that night, he warned them they would have to travel two days to reach water. The thirsty cattle would be hard to hold once they smelled water, but the herders had to keep them in control and swing the line in along the small stream or there would be bedlam. Everyone looked very somber when he finished.

"This will be a trial for our trip north next spring," he said. "There's a new cattle market in Kansas. Should have less trouble with rustlers and gangs going up there that way."

Everyone nodded in approval.

"Bet there's Indians galore, I figure, going up. They ain't all Comanche bad, but we'll pass by them. Plus the frontiers always got men that would rather steal than work. I want every man armed from here on. I want you to shoot some ammo so you can hit a bull in the ass anyway."

The crew chuckled, and they teased each other around the circle.

"This is serious. We'll be in Comanche country all winter. Always two men stay together. Always have your guns loaded and ready. Shoot first and ask questions later. Everyone savvy?"

He checked their solemn nods in the campfire's orange light around the ring. Slocum looked them over hard. Some of those young faces wouldn't be there when they reached Abilene. He hoped it was a minimum number that wouldn't be there.

Horses bucked in the predawn light as the hands prepared to ride out. With mesquite wood smoke in his nose, Slocum drank his coffee from a tin cup. He'd sent Shorty to scout the way an hour earlier. He'd told him he wanted no part of that abandoned Indian camp in case the inhabitants had had a disease. Shorty was to find a way clear of that place, and to leave some small white rags tied high in the mesquite brush at intervals so the rest of them could follow the route.

Mary and her small bundle came by. They were to ride in the double cart hitched with two teams. The other carts were to follow.

"Tomas can drive them. Have a nice day," he said to her.

"You too. It's time to move on."

He handed Rosa his empty cup and nodded to Mary. "We'll be there in less than a week."

"Good." Her smile warmed him and brought back memories of the lust the night before. It had been a real homecoming celebration, and his eyelids had had the droops as the sun came up and the crew began to shape the herd with their whistling and the snap of bullwhips. *Get them critters rolling—move on!*

The packed-up wagons began to leave an hour later. He told Tomas to stay to the east of the herd's boiling dust. They'd pass the cattle by midday, and he'd join them then and show them the way.

"It's going to be two days of hell—but we should be in good shape after these first two."

Tomas smiled broadly. "*Sí, patrón.* I will guard them."

"Good." He rose in the stirrups and Mary leaned over the side for his kiss.

They were off.

Slocum reined Roan away from the rig and short-loped him toward the rising brown cloud of bellowing dust. Day one on the trail had begun. Earlier, he'd seen Hertz mark it in the ledger: "July 19th, 1866. WE START THE HERD FOR MASON."

The moon would be near full that night. So moving the cattle even at a slow pace should be easy enough. But could the men hold up for two days in the saddle? It was a real test. He'd have coffee and food breaks set up. They'd need fresh horses. There were so many things to think about, he felt panicked inside his guts that he'd miss one.

A cinch broke, dumped his rider, Toledo. The horse then ran off and the vaquero had to ride double with Jose. Slocum rode back and found the horse dragging reins. He tried twice to catch him by riding in, and in the end lost his patience when the horse bolted the second time. Loosening his lariat, he rode the pony down and roped him. Then he backtracked until he discovered the saddle—grateful Toledo had put it high in the mesquite for him to find it.

He short-loped Roan back to the herd and took a spare girth from his saddlebags. Toldeo bounded off and he worked the right side, while Slocum worked the left. They soon had the saddle cinched down.

A big grateful smile flashed on the drover's face. He charged off to join the crew. Slocum remounted Roan and continued his surveillance of the riders. The cattle were holding good in the file. No doubt the yoking process had broken some of the wild will in many of them. They still were little more than deer being driven to a place they'd never seen.

At the midday break when they let the steers spread out and graze, Juan brought in the remuda for the riders to take fresh horses. Matilda had coffee and beef wrapped in tortillas for them as they took turns filing in and back. Several took their spell napping too.

"So far so good, amigo," Paco said, squatted on his heels beside Slocum.

"Going good. Matilda says the wagons are moving northward and should easily make camp where I said for them to before sundown. There are many things to do on such a large drive. I've made some smaller drives during the war to get beef to the troops with a lot more help than we have."

Paco nodded as if in deep thought. "Good thing you know some of these things. I'm sure learning lots."

"More burritos?" Matilda asked.

Both men thanked her and smiled. "You are doing good," Slocum said to her.

"Mary, she is the one who helps me so much. She organizes everything and carries that baby like he's part of her. She is a great *madre*."

Slocum nodded. Another time, another place—it might have worked for the two of them. He still wasn't certain his ploy in Arkansas to substitute his friend's corpse for his own had worked. He was uncertain enough not to make any permanent ties with anyone. Only time would tell.

He rubbed his whisker-bristled mouth and sucked on an eyetooth. Time would either be in his favor or against him. Texas and the West were a vast land, but since he had been a Confederate, there was always some bitterness left over that would make him a target regardless of what happened in Van Buren, Arkansas.

"You know I may not be on that drive to Kansas with you."

Paco wheeled around on his left leg to peer at him with a look of shock. "Why, amigo?"

"There ain't everything settled over my shoulder."

"But—but—"

"That boy I brought back with me, Hertz, will grow into being your bookkeeper. He's smart and learns fast. He can do the numbers and find the credit if I'm not here. You go back and build a ranch. No white man will challenge you for it for years. Buy the land from the state of Texas. They will sell it cheap. But you know how to use it."

Paco shrugged and turned his calloused palms up. "But that sounds so com-plie-cated to me."

"Speak to Hertz. We will train him to think Estrella Ranchero."

"Oh, if you would only stay. You—me, we make a good team, no?"

"I'll get you set up at Mason. Then I need to go learn about Heck's strongbox in Fort Worth."

"I almost forgot that key."

Slocum nodded. "Better get a siesta. In a little while we'll be up all night."

By the following dawn, Slocum's eyes felt like two hot sand holes. The cattle's hoarse bawling increased—they were thirsty and a long way from quenching it.

Shorty came back and joined the crew. "Plenty of water west of that camp. It's been pilfered since you were there. The pelts and anything valuable's been taken."

No surprise. Slocum nodded as they rode on the east side

of the herd. The file, four to five steers wide in a long ribbon, was obscured by the boiling red brown dust. The earth thundered from four thousand hooves, horns clacked, and the cattle's bawls carried over the land in a constant symphony that rang in his ears.

Only one horse went lame, and another was secured. Paco rode swing rider for an hour until Montag got his fresh mount. Slocum wondered when Juan led him off if the limping bay pony would have to be turned loose. The two female drovers did their part, riding hard, keeping the breakouts from escaping, and driving them back into the herd. The entire crew worked like a team on the second day, despite no sleep the night before, and in mid-afternoon, Slocum heard the change in the cattle's bawl.

Water—they'd smelled it. This would be the test. The voices of the herd had changed. How they'd smelled water in that dust bowl surrounding them he'd never know, but now they had the scent of it. The real challenge was coming. Momentum began to gather. The swing riders needed to move apart as he'd told them.

The closer they funneled the herd, the faster they went. A wider throat at the head of the drive should slow them down and allow the two swing riders to make the turn east, then back west, so the cattle lined the stream and didn't pile into a sea of horns in the shallow waterway. He charged Big John for the point of the herd, knowing Paco was up there too.

"You hear them?" he shouted, riding full tilt beside his partner as they swept the galloping herd to the east.

"The minute they smelled it like you said," Paco shouted back.

"We need to start swinging them north again."

"*Sí.*" Paco shouted in Spanish to Montag a few yards ahead. "Circle them to the west."

The swing rider, cracking his short bullwhip as he rode full tilt, reached up and waved his sombrero at his opposite rider. Then he pushed his bay horse hard at the leaders, and they began to turn. Like a well-oiled instrument, the long coil of cattle was turning, and would soon be drinking up and down the small stream with little struggle.

Slocum reined up with a wave of relief going over him. After two days in the saddle, the drovers were working like a well-oiled machine. Why, they'd make it to Kansas or even Canada. He'd stop worrying about them.

Sawing at his horse's mouth, Paco slid in close. "We did it, amigo."

Slocum rose in the stirrups, rode over, and clapped him on the shoulder with a cloud of dust. "Damn right."

That evening, he dropped in his blankets before sundown, and was up at midnight sipping coffee for his turn at riding night herd. Half-asleep, he took from Juan the reins to a horse selected for that job. One who avoided stepping on sleeping cattle and stampeding the rest. The hot coffee tasted bitter, but he'd drunk two cups blaming the gyp water for the bad flavor.

At the herd, he sent Toledo back to sleep.

"We ain't going but ten miles in the morning," he said to the sleepy drover.

"Far enough for me." Toledo rode off in the starry night in a long jog slumping like a flour sack in the saddle.

Three days later, at mid-morning, Shorty rode in and told him they'd be at Miller Creek by mid-afternoon. Slocum slumped in the saddle over the news. He'd known they would be close, and had talked about it that morning, but the scout riding in with the news made him feel relaxed. One more job about done.

Shorty shoved his hat back and frowned. "But I seen some scattered horse shit."

"You see anything else?"

"Nope. But the Texas Rangers say that's a pretty sure sign of Injuns. A loose horse shits in a pile."

"Makes sense. In the morning I'm riding into Mason and getting us some rifles and some blasting power."

"Blasting powder?"

"I learned how to use it in the war. It'll be a good aid in case we need it."

"You thinking like I am. We ever can teach them Comanche we ain't fooling, they'll make a wide berth around us."

"A little boy gets burned, he respects fire."

"You sound like my maw."

Slocum chuckled. "We may have a real fandango tonight."

"Yes, I'll ride up and check on the ranch headquarters," Shorty said. "The women and carts will be getting there in a little while."

"Hold up. I'm going along. I ain't sure about that well. May need to be cleaned out before we use it."

"Sure."

They set out short-loping to the north. Met Paco and told him their plans, and then rode on.

In a short while, they passed the train with a wave, crossed a wide grassy stretch, and went over a rise; then Shorty pointed it out on the horizon. A flag waved about the jacales. It was the flag of the Confederacy. Both men shut down their horses.

Slocum peered in the distance through his sun-squinted eyes. *What in the hell is that about?*

19

Slocum sat his horse and faced the guard wearing the gray forage cap and toting a brass-cased Henry rifle.

"Kin I help yeah?" the cocky-looking boy, hardly out of his teens, said, aiming the rifle at him.

"Go get the colonel," Slocum said, recognizing the sentry from his stopover for a drink at Fort McKay.

He shook his head. "Colonel don't like his naps disturbed. He figured you'd be along this afternoon. Said for me to blow your ass off if you tried anything like taking this place."

"I guess the colonel figured you were dispensable."

"What de hell is dat?"

"Means he figured you'd make good target practice for Shorty and me."

"By Gawd—" He shoved the muzzle of the rifle at Slocum.

"You've got thirty seconds to shoot or die." He used his spur to gouge Big John on the far side to get him ready to leap forward. Reins holding him in check, the big gelding began to step up and back making the guard blink at him in a confused fashion.

"I'll shoot yeah—I will—I swear—"

"Heeyah!" Slocum screamed, and the gelding jumped

forward striking the youth with its chest. The rifle went off in the sky. Slocum leaned over and busted the youth over the head with his pistol butt. His knees went down and he crumpled on the ground.

Shorty, with his .44 in his hand, searched the low wall from end to end, then shook his head. "Nothing else."

"Oh, they're here," Slocum said, stepping down and taking the rifle and the guard's handgun from the holster. He jammed the revolver in his waistband, and he swung back up on the horse with the Henry over his lap. What did Colonel Iram Williams have in mind?

"I figured so. How'd you know he wouldn't shoot?"

"His eyes. He'd never shot anyone. There's a look in every shooter's eyes. I've seen it too many times—"

"Who the hell's out here shooting?" The colonel's tall frame filled the doorway of the second jacal. Sleepy-eyed, he emerged, and the other two came from the next jacal.

"Better tell them to ease their hands off them gun butts," Slocum said. "You're going to be the first dead man on the scene when the firing starts."

"They'll kill you."

Slocum shook his head. "Not before you're on the way to no-man's land."

"This is my place now." The colonel ran his left hand over his mouth.

"You got a deed?"

"Sure." He started to turn to go inside.

"Ease off that. We'll both go look at it." Slocum stepped down and with his eyes on the other two, nodded to Shorty. "Kill 'em if they try a thing."

"I can do that."

Inside the jacal, the colonel went to his coat and carefully removed a folded paper. "Here's the deed. Signed, sealed, and delivered—"

The deed was in his left hand and he tried to shove it at Slocum's right hand. Instead, he got a gun barrel in his gut, and the washed-out look on his face in the shadowy light told Slocum enough. Williams's plan to jump him had failed

"One of us," Slocum said through his clenched teeth, "is fixing to die."

He unfurled the paper and turned it to the light. The paper read: "I Sam Brown of sound mind and body do grant the Bar C Ranch to Iram Williams. Signed with a big X."

"It ain't legal. No metes and bounds."

"By damn, it will hold in court."

"Load your stuff up and take it out of here. And if you ever come out here and harass the Estrella bunch, I'll hunt you down and shoot your ass off." He made the point with his gun muzzle, jabbing it hard enough to draw a grunt out of the man.

"You won't—"

"Don't threaten me, Williams. I'd as soon kill you right here as later." Slocum jerked the man's pistol out of his holster, and then shoved him with his gun barrel toward the doorway.

"I'll be back with a sheriff's order of eviction."

"I may tree him too. Now get. Oh, and take down that flag. I don't want any bluebellies thinking I'm starting another war."

"I ain't through fighting the sonsbitches." Williams scowled at him.

"That's where we differ. But you come back, I'll damn sure have a war with you."

"Get the flag," the colonel said, coming outside and putting on his felt hat. The hatless sentry ran to obey him.

"I want his rifle back." Williams indicated the Henry that Slocum had set by the door when going in to see the "deed."

"He ought not to have pointed it at me."

"He had orders to kill you."

"My daddy always said don't send a boy when you need a man. I'll keep that gun. Now tell that boy to bring your things outside. One misstep and he dies with you."

"Randy, get my things," Williams said to the youth.

"Yes, sir."

"Can the others get their horses?" Williams asked.

"No, Randy can get them. Everyone stay at ease right where you are."

The youth, out of breath, brought out the colonel's bedroll and things. Then he set them down and ran off for their horses.

"I'll not take this without protest."

"Williams, you figured I'd pay you for the use of this rat trap or you'd squeeze something out of me for its use. You can protest all you want—that X on the paper is not the owner."

"Said he was."

"He lied to you. This place belongs to the state of Texas. I already checked it out before I rode south to get the herd. The purchase price was never completely paid by the Tucker family, so they defaulted according to the county clerk."

"We'll see." Williams was breathing hard through his nose.

"Williams, maybe you should ride on. This country ain't big enough for both of us."

"We'll see."

"No, my dollar paid down and my pledge to pay the full price for it in one year will hold it that long."

"What's the price?"

"One thousand dollars. Shorty, you gather all their guns. We may need them if they want to come back looking for trouble."

"Yes, sir. I was wondering when you'd get around to that." He bailed off his horse and went to disarming them.

"I still think you're bluffing." Williams scowled hard at Slocum under the blazing sun.

"Williams, I'm not the man to mess with. I've had enough. Another word out of you and you four can walk back to where you came from."

"We'll see."

"I got the horses," Randy said, out of breath. He held the reins on the four of them.

"Well, saddle them then," the colonel said in anger.

"Yes, sir."

In ten minutes, the angry crew rode out the gate headed

for Mason. Slocum stood with Shorty at the gate and they watched Williams's departure. Then the bells of the approaching train rang out in the distance. Slocum nodded in approval at their coming.

"I never knew you went to the courthouse to ask about this place," Shorty said, raising his hat and scratching his scalp.

"Sounded official enough, didn't it?"

"It sure did." Shorty began to chuckle, then laughed till he bent over. "Man, it was a real bluff if I ever heard one."

"Williams will be a few days figuring it out."

"Then what?"

"Possession is nine tenths of the law."

"What's that mean?"

"That we've got a good chance of staying here till spring."

"That's all we need."

"Right."

"Beats the hell out of me. We've got three new Henry rifles, one more Spencer, and four pistols. That's about enough to defend it."

"Some ammo, and we'll be set."

Shorty narrowed his eyes and looked at the western crest. "What about them scattered horse apples I been finding?"

"Let's see. We've made enemies of Williams, there's a killer called Matt who done in the crew, and a couple thousand Comanches want us to fail. I'd say the odds are good we're going to have more problems."

"You know something?" Shorty said as the first cart with Mary and Tomas aboard came through the gate with them waving and shouting all excited about the new place.

"What's that?" Slocum turned to him.

"I never for one minute felt any fear facing that guard or them fellas."

Slocum nodded. *He didn't fear much either. But when it came, it cramped his guts.*

20

In the darkness of the jacal, shaved, bathed, and clean, he lay with his arm across Mary's bare stomach and fondled her left breast. Outside, the fandango music still filled the night, the big celebration showed no signs of wearing down. Alone at last in their own small jacal, with Baby Heck asleep, Slocum was itching for a night of lovemaking with her.

She clutched his hand that massaged her breast. "Oh, I feel so good to be clean at last."

"Guess I'll mess that all up."

"No. That's why I'm so clean—for you." She rolled in his direction.

He raised up and kissed her hard on the mouth, feeling her smooth flesh against his, the rock-hard pockets of her breasts under his chest as she turned onto her back with him going along, her fingers combing through his hair and her breathing hard through her nose as their tongues sought each other. The world began to swirl in his brain. His need for her started to rise like a mercury thermometer soared up when plunged in a boiling pot. His palm began to slide over the tight skin on her hip and the mound of her butt, pulling her closer against him.

Under him, his erection began to rise and poke her belly. He slipped between her silky legs as she parted them for him. His emerging hard-on began to throb with power, and he arched his back to prepare for his entry. Reaching under him with her small hand, she guided his spear to the gates of her lubricated cunt. At his entry, she gave a small cry of pleasure and clutched his upper arms, then arched her back until he was against the bottom.

Then he began to pump it to her. Her hair spilled around her face as the soft moans of pleasure escaped her slightly open lips as he braced himself over her. They were headed for heights never before attained. From the top of that pinnacle, he wanted their glide back to reality to last forever. Harder. Faster. Wilder. Walls began to contract. The drum-tight skin on the head of his swollen dick felt ready to burst. Her clit rubbed like a pencil stub on top of his shaft with each plunge. The effort by both of them was coming out in grunts. Straining, driving, hunching hard to wrench the last drop of pleasure out of each stroke. Then her fingernails dug in the skin on his upper arms and she clung to him for dear life as her butt levered off the pallet and she pushed so hard.

He exploded inside her. Twin needles pierced him in both cheeks of the ass. Then a powerful force squeezed his testicles so hard, the pain flashed to his brain and forced his hips to shove deep into her for the second hot flush that filled her with his cum.

He lay beside her. Dazzled and dumb. Exhausted and spent. Then his eyes closed, and he never awoke till late in the night with her back curled to his belly. His half-deflated dick, he discovered, was still in her. He put it in her a little deeper, and closed his eyes. *All right.*

Slocum made a trip with Paco to meet Goldman and discuss their current needs—flour, coffee, cornmeal, raisins, dried apples, lard, bacon, canned tomatoes, salt, sugar, and baking soda. As well as ammo for their weapons and two kegs of black powder, plus lead to mold bullets for the revolvers. The rifles took rimfire ammo, and the two men took several cases back with them. Slocum asked several folks around Mason about Colonel Williams, but no one said anything about him. He decided the colonel might have gone to the fort to lick his wounds. He even met the county sheriff, a man by the name of Allen. He looked harmless enough—he didn't even carry a piece. Slocum could not understand all the farmers and people in the town who never even took a weapon with them in the buggy or wagon when they went somewhere. They didn't take the Comanche threat as seriously as he did.

He and Paco drove back the wagon filled with the goods, and were satisfied they had enough supplies for months. Days passed uneventfully through the late summer; things went to drier and hotter as August slipped by. Then some moisture came off the gulf in the form of thunderstorms and drenched them. All the roofs leaked, and that put all hands on roof repair. With one storm right after the other sweeping in and even the dry washes running, they worked hard relining the roofs with new canvas and mudding them in. By October, they had the leaks about corrected, though the rain still found some leaks. But the country greened up and the cattle looked a lot better with their bellies full and licking the hair in swirls on their sides and back.

Cowboys went out in pairs, well armed, and relocated the strays back to the Bar C range. Shorty rode in one day and reported a big herd was coming from the south. He said the owner, Jake Cooke, wouldn't agree to turn west and avoid the Bar C range, despite asking him nice.

At daylight, Slocum put everyone in the saddle and they drove every head they could find to the east of the headquarters. Then he stationed his riders on the crests for Cooke's passing. The big herd came through headed north. A tough-looking head man rode up to Slocum and gave him a once-over.

"Kinda edgy, ain't you, mister?" the middle-aged man asked in a condescending tone.

"Kinda," Slocum said, not intimidated. "I'm just making sure you have all your cattle when you get through here—"

"You accusing me of rustling?"

Slocum shook his head. "Not my cattle."

The man twisted the end of his handlebar mustache. "I've left tougher ones than you for the buzzards to pick."

"I don't doubt it, 'cept today you wouldn't make it back to the herd. One of my boys would put a .44 bullet in your back. No gain in your herd passing through here either."

"What the hell's your name?"

"Slocum."

"Jake Cooke. We'll cross trails again."

"Jake Cooke, next time my man asks you to skirt west of our place, you better heed his advice."

"Or what?"

"I'll plant a cross over you."

"I'll see you in Bonner Springs next spring. We can settle it there."

"We might do that."

Cooke gave him a hand wave, turned the big horse westward, and rode off for his herd.

Paco rode in and slid his pony to a stop. "What did he say?"

"Said he'll see me in Bonner Springs next spring."

"What for?" Paco frowned after the man, who was almost to the dust of his own bunch.

"To kill me."

"You going to Bonner Springs?"

"No, I'm going to Abilene."

Paco slapped his large flat horn and shook with a belly laugh. "How long is he going to wait for you there?"

"Till hell freezes over, I guess. What he tried was called the big sweep. He rides through and gets all the cattle he can in his herd, then blots the brand before they arrive at the market."

"Plenty of bad hombres, ain't there?"

"Plenty. But we outfoxed one. Now we need to make some traps. The next full moon, the Comanches will ride down and make raids."

"What kind of traps?"

"I'll show you what I mean."

Matilda had saved and washed all the airtight cans for him. He took one that afternoon, filled it with black powder, set it on a rise, then ran a primer cord with a primer attached to the end of it and buried it in the black powder. A hundred feet away, he struck a match and they watched the cord spark across the ground. They were all shouting until the can blew up in the largest explosion of smoke and powder they'd ever seen or heard, which made them all draw back.

"That's a Comanche chaser. It'll make their horses go wild and panic. They won't wait for many more to go off. Who can throw a stick of blasting powder that far?"

"I can," Toledo said, and came forward.

Slocum handed him a bundle of sticks that weighed as much as a stick of blasting powder. The drover reared back, ran three steps, and the package was launched high in the sky. It landed less than ten feet from the explosion site.

"You get that job." Slocum nodded and tossed a whiskey bottle to Tomas. "Put it on that rise out there."

Tomas took off in small cloud of dust, his sandals churning up dirt.

"Now one shot at a time. I want to see the real shooter who can bust that bottle. Either a Spencer or Winchester."

"Can I shoot?" Hertz asked.

"Sure, you're one of us."

The youth took a Spencer, set the sight leverage at thirty yards, kneeled down, looked hard through the sights, and squeezed off a shot. The bottle flew in a thousand pieces and Hertz looked around at the awed crowd. "Who's next?"

Paco squeezed his chin and shook his head in disbelief. "That boy could kill a fly down there."

"Tomas, put up a new bottle. Who's next?"

The crowd began to applaud and nod their heads in approval of Hertz's shooting. He swept off his small black hat for them as he went back to his wife. She smiled and hugged him with pride. Slocum knew the boy with the hard-to-understand accent had just found his place on the crew.

"Me." Shorty stepped forward, picked up the same rifle, chambered in a shell. He took aim at the new one and busted the neck off it. More applause.

So the afternoon went, but no one else a busted bottle

like Hertz had. Even the four women shot rifles. Matilda and Mary hit the target after some coaching. The other two shot wild enough that Slocum excused them from rifle practice.

He cut the distance down and the crew had pistol practice on an array of bottles. They all could shoot, and some were crack shots. The plan for the Comanches was laid out. Paco made a new clapper for the old ranch bell; then he used a wet rawhide wrap to reinforce the loose nails that held it on the post. A new pull rope, and the alarm was ready. When it went to ringing, they were to come in and support the ranch's defense.

Each night Juan brought in the remuda. That was what the Comanches would steal first. Each morning, the youth and a guard armed with a rifle went to grazing with them. Each night they came in long before sundown.

Slocum sipped on his morning coffee as the horses went out in a long jog. November was a good month for the warriors to come in during the full moon of the gray goose. The honkers had been going over for a week. The boys had shot some low-flying ones for the table. Paco, Tomas, and Juan had ridden into the hill country and shot six deer. The cool night kept them fresh enough while the women jerked the meat, pounded it with pumice with the wild plums they'd picked and dried earlier. Stored in leather bags and sealed under four inches of beef tallow, it was the Mexican version of pemmican and could stay fresh for years.

They also picked and shelled mesquite beans.

Hertz asked Slocum about the steers. Were any broken well enough to make teams?

"Why?"

"Many of the farmers need teams of oxen. They don't have money, but they would barter trade."

"Like what?"

"Oh, I could get four barrels of flour for a gentle team."

"We'll have a meeting tonight. Some of them would make ox—they really tamed down yoked up. They'd get calm again yoked for a while, I figure. Let's talk to Paco. I'm excited."

His partner blinked at the idea later that evening. "Sell oxen?"

"Yes, lots of these farmers need teams. No cash, but they have commodities we can use."

"Yes, that would be wonderful, huh, amigo?"

"Best idea we've come across."

"We will cut out several steers in the morning. I think we can find gentle ones." Paco looked at Slocum, who agreed.

The roundup began the next morning, and Hertz drove into Mason to post a sign at Goldman's. OXEN TEAMS IN EX- CHANGE FOR PRODUCE. BAR C RANCH.

All the steers they drove in were not as willing to resub- mit to yoking, and the dust flew in the corrals. Cattle bawled and bucked. The gentler ones were kept, the wild ones run out the front gate. Soon, the competition to find the right ones and drive them in from the range became keen among the two-person teams.

The first purchaser brought four barrels of fine-sifted flour to trade. At twenty bucks a barrel on the credit, Slocum was backing Hertz's ambition to find Mr. Gomer a fine team for his flour. Gomer didn't like the first team they showed him—too small. The second one they drove into the arena was too tall and would eat too much feed. Paco found the next team, a shorter, blocky pair, to drive into the pen for Gomer to inspect. Gomer's arms folded over his black suit coat and he made a great nod of approval at the sight of them.

Slocum nodded to Mary—they had four precious barrels of flour.

Another farmer, named Berner, sent Hertz word he wanted two of the tamest steers and would pay four hundred pounds of dried frijoles for them if they were tame. The tamest two were not the best matched, one was a few inches taller than the other. The man in his white shirt, funny black hat, and black suit delivered the beans in his oxcart. He walked around them and appraised them tied to the fence while the ranch crew looked on. He put his hands on them and they chewed their cud placidly. Relief went through everyone when he decided they were tame enough and he nodded his approval to Hertz.

Herr Berner drove them out of the arena, took a chain hitched to the back of his Red River cart, and attached it to the yoke. He didn't give the new steers much slack. When they were tied on and dancing some on their toes, Herr Berner went around to his own team, flicked the whip, and said, "Get up" in German.

They left the Bar C, and the new steers were either going to go along or be dragged, the onlookers could see. They didn't go willingly, and even skidded as they left. Slocum figured by the time the pair reached Mason, they'd be used to *oxdom*. The second trade really opened the all-new business—swapping for oxen.

The next team brought two barrels of dry apples. The crew was scouting every day for more potential draft teams out of the herd. A year's supply of raisins came next for a solid black team, which was all Herr Gruder would accept. They traded two teams for some good barrels of wine. Slocum had begun to believe there was no end to this oxen business. A trade was made for a barrel of sauerkraut and two woolen sweaters. Matilda got one sweater because she was always cold, and Darla, who had begun to show her coming baby, got the second one. Besides, Hertz was doing the biggest share of the trading.

Slocum was beginning to believe the Comanche had accepted his force at the ranch. They weren't the kind of Indians to meet the army on the battlefield, but small bands made incursions and raids. Isolated ranches poorly defended, herders, lone travelers, and small wagon trains all were the targets of their raids. They went as far south as central Mexico's north provinces to make raids on unarmed villages and isolated haciendas—gaining captives, horses, supplies, and loot.

Shorty rode in one bleary morning to Slocum's jacal.

"More sign today. Several horses passed west of here last night."

"Ride out and tell Juan to bring in the horses. They're better off hungry than stolen," Slocum said from the doorway

"Sure thing, boss."

"What's going on?" Paco asked.

"Shorty cut lots of sign over west this morning. I'm calling in the horses until we know more."

"What are we going to do?"

"Saddle up and go scout for them."

Paco grinned. "You know, I was getting bored laying around here."

"Bring a rifle, we may have all the excitement we need if we do find them."

"Tomas, catch the horses Juan left for us today."

"*Sí, patrón.*" The youth ran off to get them.

"Be ready in minutes," Slocum said. He went back inside and squatted by the fire. With a kerchief for a pot holder, he refilled his coffee cup. Mary sat cross-legged sewing a buckskin seat in his other pair of britches. She met his gaze.

"They finally came, huh?"

"Maybe. I'll be back." He looked at little Heck sitting atop a blanket next to Mary, playing with a smooth bone he could chew on.

"He and I'll be waiting," she said.

"Take care of her, little man." He rose, kissed her on top of the head, then went for his gun and hat. "Don't wait up."

"We'll be here."

He nodded and went outside. A buttermilk sky shut off the sun. He jammed the rifle in the scabbard. There were half a dozen tubes of ammo sticking out of his bags. He tossed up the stirrup and checked the girth. Then he swung aboard and headed for Paco. *Comanche time.*

21

"How bad are you hit?" Slocum shouted to Paco over his shoulder as he spurred his horse hard and gave him rein with his left hand.

"My left arm. I can ride. Go!"

For a second, he hesitated, then shook his head in disapproval. "'Ride like hell. There's too damn many of them for us to fight them here."

"I'm coming—"

Damn. They'd found a whole band of them. Their hair-raising screaming and yipping like coyotes told him the war party was coming hard, and they were over a mile away from the Bar C compound. He'd never wanted to test his drilling of the crew on what to do like this. What worried him the most was how he and Paco could make it to the ranch.

"Go off there." He pointed. Paco never argued, and reined his pony off the side with him. They took their horses off a steep bank into a dry wash. A ploy Slocum hoped would confuse them. But sliding down the bank, he saw more angry painted faces and screaming Comanches coming from the left down the wash at them.

He managed to turn the horse he rode, and so did Paco. They tore down the dry bed. No need to shoot at them, he'd never hit one. His heart in his throat, he lashed the pony to go faster and they charged the hill. How many bucks were there, a hundred? Fifty? Sounded like ten thousand of them all screaming—making bloodcurdling noises all around them. But their hard-breathing horses were maintaining a distance that kept the bow hunters out of range. Then he could see the outline of the ranch headquarters. He spurred and whipped the bay harder. The animal gave a surge, and Paco's mount on his right did the same, like they knew the ranch might save them too.

Slocum chanced a glance back. He could see a black-faced buck on a fast paint with a lance charging in the lead. That Comanche wanted one of them on his stabber. Slocum drew his pistol and cocked it—he might not hit the buck, but if he shot the horse, he'd stop him. How did they get in this mess anyway?

Shot one. Nothing. The brave had his horse wound up and was gaining. This shooting off a galloping horse might be foolish. Maybe he should be making his horse run faster. He snapped off another shot—no results. Time to cut or shoot. He twisted more this time in the saddle. Took aim and fired. The paint went nose-down in the dirt, his rider under him, and the lance spilled away.

His wreck caused a pileup of horses and Comanche. Slocum glanced back at the diversion—might be what they needed.

"*Madre de Dios!* You stopped him." Paco went to urging his mount on faster.

"If they don't open that gate, we'll have to jump the wall," Slocum shouted over the wind in his face at his partner, who was riding stride for stride beside him.

"I can't pull him up enough with one good arm."

"Better hope they move the carts in the gate then."

Paco, white-faced and strained-looking, nodded. They charged on. Arrows whizzed by them. It was serious. The war party didn't want them to make it to the ranch. Those screaming bucks were getting real worked up about that in Slocum's estimation. Less than a quarter mile left and both of their horses were running out of steam. Slocum could feel his pony losing speed.

The distance cut in half, and Slocum saw the people at the ranch pull the carts aside and leave a space for them to enter. He could hear their people screaming for them to hurry. Hell, they were doing all they could.

They both stood in the stirrups and drew the last bit left in their mounts. A war-painted buck aboard a wide-mouthed lathered horse swept in beside Slocum. His ax's blade flashed in the sun. Slocum knew he'd never draw his gun in time to stop him and stay on his own horse. The brave swung his war ax at him. Slocum ducked and the brave missed. When he drew back again, a bullet from the compound stopped him in midair and he pitched out of the saddle.

Slocum and Paco hit the gate and set down their horses in the yard. "Mary, see about Paco. He's been shot."

He jerked his Spencer out of the scabbard along with several tubes from the saddlebags, and ran to the wall. When he reached the barrier, an explosion went off behind the mob of Comanches milling around on lathered horses. It bolted many of their mounts toward the wall and put them in easy gun range. The ranch rifles opened up. Then more blasting sticks thrown at them sent Indians and horses flying and the dust grew thicker. Slocum picked off targets he could see—horses or riders. No time to be particular.

Then there was no more screaming, only horses in pain. Many animals lay in the field thrashing as the wind began to clear the dust away. The braves were gathered back farther away on their horses as if considering another charge. The blasting powder had made enough of an impression on them to take notice.

Slocum looked up and down the line at the dust-floured faces of the crew and women. "Anyone wounded?"

"No. 'Cept Paco."

"Good."

"They want more?" Toledo asked, ready with more armed blasting sticks.

"They're deciding that now."

"You wish you had a cannon?" Shorty asked.

"We could sure use one. Couple of you run out there and get a few bows and arrows off those dead ones out there. I've got an idea."

He cut a couple of sticks of blasting powder in half, armed them with a blasting cap and fuse, then tied the first one on an arrow. "Give me the biggest bow."

"All right," he said, drawing back the bow they brought him to test. "Here goes our Indian cannon. Light it."

He aimed high and the smoking charge made a tall arch. It exploded close to the ground and sent the Comanches running for their lives on equally frightened horses. His actions drew laughter from everyone.

"They thought they were safe out there," Montag said. "Now they know better."

"Comanches are like hornets, boys," Slocum said as Paco, with his left arm in a sling, came from the jacal. "Sometimes you only make them madder."

"All our horses are in here and everyone is accounted for?" he asked.

"So far so good."

"What now, *general*?" Paco teased with his arm in a sling. "Your army is ready, no?"

"They ain't done bad so far. How are you?"

"I have a hole in my arm. The bullet went through. I think it will be fine."

Mary nodded and came over for Slocum to hug her. "He doesn't get an infection, he'll be fine."

Slocum nodded, and tried to see the Indians through the distant dust churned up by their horses and the wind. Rosa brought a pot of coffee, and the shy girl Gato gave them each a cup. He thanked the two and sipped on his with Mary close by.

"I saw you two coming and those-those killers right on your heels—I thought you might not make it."

"Hey, the Good Lord saved me and Paco was all."

She shook her head in disapproval.

He squeezed her shoulder and kissed her forehead. "Mary, how can you doubt me?"

"You're bad, Slocum—bad."

"Paco, we got any whiskey?"

"No. We got some wine."

"Let's all have a drink and settle down. There is no telling what they'll do next. Just a few glasses of wine. Don't get drunk. They ain't done with us yet."

He looked off to the south. They were still milling around down there. *No telling.*

22

Whether they had tired of the game or thought better of it, the Comanche had moved on. Slocum stood in the quiet predawn satisfied they were gone. Earlier, he'd been out beyond the wall, and saw no signs of them. They'd even left their dead on the field. It would be a mess to clean up—but the lesser of the evils when compared to more warfare.

He wondered who was the chief of this bunch. Not that it mattered, but he'd heard many feared names. Walking Bear, Tall Man, He-Rides-Hard, all names on the frontier evoking awe and cold terror.

"You learn anything?" Hertz asked, coming with his rifle.

"No. I think they went on to easier pickings. Thanks for the good shot yesterday."

"It was nothing."

"My life is all. In the army they'd give you a medal."

"You gave me one, remember?"

"Huh?"

"Darla."

"Good enough then. But we aren't even."

"Oh, Slocum, these people here no longer think I am some dumb German boy. I am accepted now. I am one of them. I am a man, no?"

"A helluva man you've made. You made all the good

trades for the oxen. If I have to leave, you will need to help Paco with the business end."

Hertz blinked his eyes as if shocked by his words. "Where will you go?"

Slocum chewed on his lower lip. "I'm not certain. I simply might have to leave."

Hertz nodded. "I will always remember you and what you did for us. Her father was mean to her and he'd never let me marry her. I was not rich enough to suit him."

"I understood that. You remember then—there will be times that you will need to take charge of a situation and do it right."

"Yes—do it right."

In the weeks ahead, word came back. The Comanches wanted no part of the Bar C, which fought with thunder sticks. That was the gossip in Mason. Goldman told Slocum he'd heard that from a whiskey trader.

"So you must have made a real impression on them?"

Slocum shook his head. "Might only make us a bigger target they want to smash."

"True. You mean a challenge."

Slocum agreed. No telling about Indians—they could change their mind in a minute and get in a frenzy about anything. Especially full of some rotgut whiskey. The ranch hands had recovered two Spencers and four new Winchesters from the dead Indians at their gate. Someone was selling the Comanche guns and that bunch, in Slocum's eyes, needed their hides tacked to the outhouse wall.

When the moon went down in size, he set out for Fort Worth anxious to see what was in Heck Allen's lockbox. The ride took four days and before he reached Fort Worth, he wrapped his right hand in a bandage he'd secured from a small crossroad store. Signing the register like Heck might be hard, but if no one questioned him and he couldn't write— his plan might work. With Roan stabled, he went directly to the Texas State Bank and presented himself as Heck Allen.

The man with small glasses who sat behind the lockbox service desk acted bored when Slocum told him his business. He had him sign an X that he witnessed, looking with disdain at the bandaged hand, and then showed him back to the vault. The small box was withdrawn and set on the small table in the great vault. The man said he'd put it back if Slocum couldn't, and left him.

Inside the metal box was a deed to a hundred and forty acres, some jewelry that must have been Heck's mother's, and a letter.

In the event I have died, to whoever reads this—there is five hundred dollars in gold coins buried on Laney Crick. It came from the Riely, Texas, bank robbery— you can return it to them or spend it—suit yourself. Heck Allen.

Slocum looked at the map. Shouldn't be hard to find. A shovel, invest a little time, and he'd have the money. He put the deed and map inside his shirt, slid the box back in, then thanked the man going out. It was in the sunlight outside with a cold north wind sweeping his face when he finally relaxed.

It took a day to find Laney Creek and the site off the Thomasville Road. He'd secured some canvas bags and found the place was unfenced. He used a steel rod to bring some river worms up by driving it in the ground and beating on it so the vibration would send them to the surface. With an empty tin can half full of fat ones, he found an eddy and a small logjam. With a hook, line, and cane pole, he fished there for a few hours, catching a few flopping bullheads and some pan fish to be sure he wasn't drawing any attention.

"Catching a mess?" a farmhand asked, coming down from the bridge and chewing on grass stem.

"Yeah, I was raised on a crick and had to stop when I seen this one. Ain't no creeks like this out where I ranch."

"Get west of here very fur and there ain't no water."

"Right. I was just going to fish some here and fry me a mess and go on. No one'll mind if I camp here, will they?"

"Naw. Just curious. I better get home, got cows to milk. I never caught your name."

"Tom White."

"Well, nice to meet'cha, Tom." They shook hands and the man offered his name. "Isiah Nelson."

"Well, don't milk too hard."

The man laughed. "Same to you about the fishing."

"I won't," he assured the man, and swung up another fat shell cracker onto the bank. "Could you use some? I have plenty."

"Well, I might," the man said. "I'll string some on a stick. Don't want to take all you got in that tow sack."

"Help yourself."

"Mighty neighborly. My wife loves fish." Nelson strung most of them and left with two stringers, saying thanks all the way up the bank.

An hour later, Slocum uncovered the strongbox and struggled to get it out of the hole. On his knees, he used his gun butt to bust off the lock. The bright gold ten-dollar coins the size of dimes glistened in the slanted sundown light. The amount of them impressed him. With an ear to listen for anyone approaching, he soon had them bagged and the tops of the sacks tied. He replaced the box, dirt, and sod over the hole. Then, satisfied the evidence of his digging wasn't too glaring, he put the loot in his panniers to load out when he left.

After a fish supper, he went to bed early since the November days were short. The next day he was in the saddle early, loaded his packhorse, and rode out of the area.

Five days later, he led the packhorse behind Roan into the Bar C. Mary ran out to greet him wrapped in a blanket against the cold. Something in her face telegraphed to him that things weren't right.

"Oh, I was so worried about you." She looked around as if on edge. "You didn't stop in Mason, did you?"

He shook his head. "No, why?"

"Two deputy U.S marshals have been here asking questions about you."

His heart sunk. "They're in town?"

"I don't know, but we've all been worried that you'd

been arrested and that's why you weren't back."

"Amigo, amigo," Paco shouted, coming from the other jacal. "You are all right?"

Slocum nodded. "I'm fine. She told me about the law."

"Where will you go, my friend?"

"Mexico, I guess. I'm not certain."

"But we need you—"

"Let's go inside. I have some news."

"Oh, yes, what was in Heck's lockbox?" she asked, hustling them inside the jacal.

In the jacal's warm interior, he shed his canvas duster and sat the two of them down. The baby was asleep in a small crib. "This deed is to a farm south of Fort Worth. It goes to Mary. The nice couple leasing it knows you are coming to claim it. They said they'd work for you."

"But I have no—" She swept the hair from her forehead looking disturbed over the matter.

"Heck left the farm and the deed signed. I registered it in your name. He left some money too. It came from a robbery, but no one'll ever know where. It's out there on the packhorse."

"He was a bank robber?"

Slocum nodded. "Paco, I'm giving you a hundred dollars of it. You'll need things going north. There's three-fifty in the sacks for Little Heck, and don't protest. I guess I better take fifty of it and hit the trail."

"But what will we do?" Paco asked. "You are the one—"

"No, you have the crew. Have Shorty and one of the boys move her to this place when you get a weather break. Come spring, head 'em north to Abilene. You can do it, Paco."

The man dropped his head as if the world was on his shoulders. "I am a poor Mexican vaquero. How can I?"

"No, you own the Estrella Cattle Company. There'll be rivers to cross, bad men blocking the road, and there will be plenty of trouble, but you'll be in Abilene next spring with this herd. And I'll meet you there if there is any way I can and we'll celebrate in Abilene."

"It will always be half yours, *mi amigo*."

Slocum nodded and stood. "I need a fresh horse or two."

Mary rushed over and hugged him. "Must you leave now? So soon?"

"I damn sure don't want to. But those marshals will be back. Someone might have seen me riding in." If she only knew how much he had lusted for another night with her in heaven.

"Be careful. You know where Little Heck and I'll be living?"

"Yes, and you'll like the farm. I'll drop by sometime and see both of you."

"I'll be waiting."

He kissed her, and the pain in his heart felt like a cold arrow. Paco nodded, looking long-faced, and Slocum led him outside. They went to the corral.

"What horses do you want?" Paco asked.

"The least different one from the rest. That big roan Sarge will do. He looks like a hundred more, and that other brown one for a packhorse."

Tomas had joined them. "You are leaving so soon?" the out-of-breath youth asked.

"He never was here," Paco said in a low threatening voice.

"*Sí.*"

The cold north wind swept Slocum's face. He could hardly get her out of his mind. The smooth skin. The body responsive under his attack. The walls contracting like a powerful fist. Damn dreary day. Damn cold weather. Nothing was ever fair.

He took fifty gold dollars from the heavy sacks he'd carried into her jacal and left the rest with Mary to count out Paco's money. She shook her head. Tears filled her eyes. "I can never repay you for all this."

"Yes, raise that boy. Have a life of your own."

"God bless you."

He nodded with a hard knot behind his tongue. Better

leave while he still could. He was grateful the crew was out checking cattle and he didn't need to face them too. He left her and outside, took the reins from Tomas. Then he hugged Paco and clapped him on the back.

"*Vaya con Dios.*"

"Yes." He swung up and jerked the lead—Brownie came on.

A high overcast cut down the sun to a gray light spread across the greasewood sea when he rode out of the gate. Another dreary cold day in his life. *Damn.*

23

It spit snow late that afternoon. Tiny ice grains rapped on his hat and canvas coat as he pushed south. Somewhere down there far enough, it would still be summer. There would be dark-eyed señoritas on the plaza dancing around a hat to guitar music. Swirling their colorful dresses around their shapely hips, their brown cleavage rising and falling promising the beholder hard tits to suck on and possess in his palms.

He reined up and considered the Texas flag popping in the wind. He could use a drink. There wouldn't be another place for days beyond this point. He'd simply go inside, buy a bottle, and ride on. If Williams was in there—he'd do what he had to do.

On the ground, he let his sea legs come to life before he let go of the horn. Then he opened the duster and adjusted the holster. Ordinarily, he'd let the cinches looser—in this case, he wasn't certain how long he'd stay in there.

The new rough board door's latch was hard and it finally opened. When he stepped in the candlelit interior, he let his eyes adjust and walked to the bar.

"What'll it be, Señor?"

"Bottle of whiskey."

The swarthy-faced man nodded and went for one. In the

smoky back bar mirror, Slocum studied the four at the table. He saw the gold braid on the felt hat—Williams.

"You're a long ways from all them greaser buddies of yours, ain't ya?"

"They might not be as far away as you think." Slocum turned slowly and faced them.

Willams used both hands on the chair arms to push his tall frame to a standing position. "You owe us for the Bar C."

"I don't have any money." Slocum's back muscles tensed, and he noticed the bartender had set his bottle on the bar. He tried to gauge how drunk the colonel was. He sounded impaired. A slur in his words—it was always an advantage.

"Listen, you damn trash—"

"Draw your damn gun or take that back."

"I-I—"

"Colonel didn't mean nothing. He ain't no pistolero." Billy Jack jumped up and tried to turn the man away.

"Leave me alone—I—can handle this."

"No, you can't," Billy Jack insisted. "I've seen that look before."

"Colonel." Another of them took the colonel's gun arm and forced him back. "Go on, Slocum. There ain't no trouble for you here."

"Have it your way." He paid the man, took the bottle in his left hand, and went for the door.

"Gawdamnit!" Williams swore behind him. But when Slocum opened the door and looked back, they still had him restrained.

"Good day," Slocum said, and touched his hat brim with the bottle hand, then left.

Outside, he climbed on Sarge and rode off in the gathering darkness. Been nice to have had a room and a bed to sleep in. He only had that cold bitch winter to hold him in her arms until dawn.

At sunup, he crawled out of his cocoon and rolled it up. His breath made big clouds of moisture as he reloaded and saddled the pair. The sky had cleared, so he hoped for some warmth. Little developed as the sun rose in the sky. He took a few drinks out of the neck of the bottle, and it warmed him some. No firewood on the site, so he rode on gnawing jerky.

That night, he used some of the piled-up yokes he found to build a fire and boiled some coffee, but the strong wind made keeping warm impossible, so he gave up and went to bed. At dawn, he was headed south again.

He reached Rio Frio the next afternoon. Dialgo welcomed him like a long-lost brother.

"Where are the *putas*?" Slocum asked, looking around.

"One went to Mexico for Christmas. One died." He crossed himself. "Poor Marinia."

"Which one is left?"

"Farita."

"I know her. Where is she?"

"In bed. Sleeping, I think."

"Give me a bottle of red wine. I'll go wake her up."

Dialgo smiled. "That will surprise her."

Slocum nodded. "Have a boy put my horses in a shed and feed them."

"Certainly."

He took the wine bottle and glasses and ducked going through the low doorway to the hall. At Farita's door, he shouldered aside the blanket and looked in on her sleeping on the bed.

"Time for a fandango."

"I don't want one," she grumbled, rolled over, and pulled the covers over her head.

"Ah, but I have red wine and I'm ready to party."

She sat up, holding the blanket over her nakedness, and blinked her matted lashes to try and see him. "Oh, the gringo. You're back?"

"Stay under the cover. It is probably warm under there."

"*Sí.*" She took the bottle and glasses and acted excited. "When did you get here?"

"Minutes ago. I came to see you." He toed off his boots and shed his coat.

"Whew." With her teeth in the side of her small mouth,

she wrenched out the cork and spit it aside. Then the blanket slipped away and exposed her small teardrop breasts and the pointed dark nipples. She raised the bottle up and drank from the neck.

"Who needs glasses?" he said.

"I don't," she said. Some wine ran down her chin.

He shed his shirt, pants, and then his long handles as she wiped her mouth on the back of her hand and scooted over to make room for him. He climbed on the low bed, then with the covers over his legs, took the bottle. With a deep draught, he handed it back to her.

She threw her head back and drank some more. Then, with a giggle, she reached past him to put the wine on the table. Her breasts raked over his bare chest and she looked up at him when she drew back. Her brown eyes were still sleepy-looking—he kissed her hard on the mouth and dragged her still-warm body up against him.

Her arms encircled his neck as she scrambled on his lap. She replaced her lips and put her tongue in his mouth. Between them, her fingers sought his rising sword, and when she grasped it behind the head, she threw her chin back and screamed, *"Grande! Grande!"*

She dove back onto the bed beside him, rolled on her back, adjusting blankets over them, and raised her knees, acting desperate for his entry.

"Oh," she cried, wiggling on her back as he slipped his probe into her cunt. "Oh, I have missed you so much."

He began to pump it to her, and she arched her back for his deepest entry. When he reached the bottom, she cried out, "Yes. Yes." It was wild, and she contracted with each stroke that squeezed him tight. So his entry back in was tight too.

Soon the tempo of their fierce lovemaking reached such a high plane, they both were huffing for their breath. His hips ached to poke it through her. His dick felt on fire, and then the ache in his left testicle became excruciating and he came.

They collapsed in a pile and she wiggled out to get the bottle. Smiling with her hard-muscled belly sprawled over his lap, she raised the bottle and took a large drink. Then she handed the bottle to him. "More firewater. I want to fuck you all day."

"All day?" he asked, sounding taken back.

"All day."

So they did.

He spoke to Goeserman the next morning in his store and assured the man that Paco was taking the herd on to this new market in Abilene, Kansas, and would be back in the fall to pay him.

"I wish you were still there with him."

"Circumstances didn't allow it."

Goeserman nodded as if he understood. "Where're you going next?"

"Mexico."

"Be careful down there. That Matt Cotter, he calls himself Boudry now."

"Where's he at?"

"Trading whiskey to the damn Injuns last that I heard. Going back and forth across the border with whiskey and arms."

"Guns are the main things, I'd bet good money. Those Comanche made a raid on the place we were at up there. When the fight was over, we picked up brand-new rifles."

Goeserman nodded. "Some folks will do anything to make a dollar. You never found any sign of the colonel's body?"

"No. But if I ever get my hands on Boudry, I'll squeeze out of him what he did with the colonel."

"He's tough and rides with mean men."

"You have any idea where he stays?"

"No, I haven't heard much about him lately."

Satisfied that Boudry as he called himself was up to no good, Slocum went back to the cantina and found his nymph asleep in bed. He stripped off his clothing, crawled in bed, and scooted over to her. Curled around her, he eased his half-alive dick in her from behind.

She grumbled. "I missed him. Sleep." She reached back to pull him tighter to her. They slept connected till mid-afternoon.

Then she woke him up for another round. She was on all fours under him, and he was pounding her rock-hard butt, when he heard someone in the hall clear his throat. He put his hand over her mouth. "Yes?"

"Thought you'd want to know." It was Dialgo. "Word's out that Matt and his pack train crossed into Texas yesterday. Headed northwest."

"Thanks." Boudry was on the move. More vulnerable out in the open country than when he was dug in somewhere. Maybe Slocum could single him out. He owed him for killing those boys.

Her hand shot back and slapped his leg. She was impatient for him to get going again. He reached under her and fondled her breasts until she got back in the mood. They went and went, until they finally collapsed in the bed and slept till supper time.

"What are you thinking about?" she asked, reaching across the table between them for a tortilla. She was dressed in a thin cotton gown, and her dark nipples dotted the white cloth when she sat back ready to fill the wrap with frijoles and tender long-cooked beef.

"In the morning I must leave you."

She half-closed her left eye as if in pain. "I don't please you?"

"Oh, yes, you're fine. You're wonderful. But I've got business I must attend to."

"The one Dialgo told you about, huh? That bastard Matt?"

"You know him?"

"I hate him. He used to come here. He has a dick like a small dog and he is mean."

Slocum nodded and forked in a bite of his enchilada. Maybe he could find him. Leaving her slinky bed full of pussy would be a big loss and a letdown, but some things came before that—for him, getting Boudry was number one. He'd never forget the sight of those poor boys Matt'd shot down in cold blood.

•   •   •

At midday, bellied down on a ridge, he was following the movement of the mule pack train in his new binoculars. Four Red River carts pulled by double teams of oxen trailed them a few miles back. Oxen never kept up with mules. Boudry had a half-dozen armed men with the mule skinners and three men carrying rifles with the carts. Slocum had not spotted the man himself in the glass, so there might even be more pistoleros than he had seen.

They soon made afternoon camp and the cattle were turned out to graze. The horses, mules, and bell mare also were turned loose to eat what grass the land offered. If the wrangler was careless, during the night Slocum might be able to stampede their horses and mules. Then they'd have to put what they could in the carts and walk. Pistoleros made poor foot soldiers. They were thirty miles from the Rio Grande. A long walk, and there were not enough horses there—surely not enough mules—to replenish his losses.

Slocum chewed on some jerky and thought about Farita's pear-shaped breasts and squeezing them. The horses and mules would be his next move. No moon till late. He could maybe get lucky. He pulled the blanket up over his shoulder. Even with the sun out, it was cold. Still no sign of Boudry— where was he?

Before the quarter moon rose, with the stealth of a Comanche, he worked his way down the dry wash. The wrangler was dismounted and sitting somewhere under the high bank. Slocum had seen the silhouette of his horse and had worked his way around to the wash.

The horses and mules grunted in their sleep. A few stomped, and there was an occasional squeal when one bit another out of sheer meanness. The night horse, head down, snorted in the dust. Slocum stopped and held his breath. Then he heard the light snoring and moved in quickly. He struck the seated wrangler over the head hard with the butt of his gun, and the man spilled facedown. Then Slocum roped and tied him, then gagged him. With an ear to the night sounds, he sat on his haunches and regained his breath.

Nothing sounded out of place. Next, he moved to the night horse and jerked the girth tight.

In minutes, he had the bell mare moving south. The shuffle of the mules and the occasional kicking concerned him that it might wake the pistoleros as the animals filed after the mare. Then, out of habit, the horses began to shuffle along after the mules.

Slocum's heart pounded. He grasped the .44 in his right hand and craned his head around looking for any sign. None. They were moving at a good pace out through the starlit night—the mare knew the way home, all she needed was a hint. The silver bell sounded clear when he caught Sarge and Brownie up from where he had them hitched. Then, whistling and driving at the rear of the herd, he sent them all toward Mexico.

At dawn, he broke off driving them with a hard rush to make them hurry. The bell mare showed no signs of quitting short of the border—that meant the mules wouldn't quit either. The horses might tire of the game, but they were a good distance from Boudry's camp.

Satisfied the first part of his plan was a success, Slocum picked out a defensive spot on the rise and waited. Near noon, he spotted three riders in his glasses. Obviously, he must have missed a few head. One looked like Boudry. They were busy following all the tracks when they came in rifle range and he could hear Boudry cursing. ". . . sumbitch stole them was no damn Injun."

"Throw down your guns!" Slocum ordered.

They went for their pistols instead. He took aim through the raised sight and fired. Boudry was struck hard by the first bullet and fell from his horse. Slocum rose to his feet levering in a second shot, and knocked the number-two man off his pony. The third one was waving a pistol and trying to stop his spinning horse. Slocum's second try at him took him down.

Slocum was satisfied. He turned, went down the hillside, and gained his horses. He rode around and dismounted by Boudry. He knelt down beside him, and could see his shot had struck him solidly in the chest.

"What did you do to the colonel?"

"Slocum? You?"

He grasped Boudry by the vest and shook him. "Yes, it's me. What did you do with the colonel?"

"I cut off and ate his balls looking in his face while he screamed." Boudry's eyes flickered, but he never lost the mean look. Not even when his life evaporated and his head slumped to the side.

Slocum rose, walked to Sarge, and stepped in the stirrup. Let the damn buzzards have them. He never looked back when he rode off.

Farita never asked him any questions when later the next morning he climbed in the bed with her. He curled around her warm back, and she raised her legs and inserted him inside her. Then she clapped his leg as if satisfied and they slept.

Three days later, he kissed her good-bye and rode off into Mexico. In a village called Portis, he found a man he knew called Armando who owned a cantina. It was a quiet place at the foot of the mountains where the mule loads of rich ore came down from the Sierra Madres. Hard-faced men with rifles and pistols rode guard on such shipments, and they camped at Portis for one day to rest and they drank there in shifts.

Twice a week, they came down with mule trains. Highly paid, they had enough money for whiskey and pussy. They all wore tan uniforms and stiff-brimmed four-peak hats with chin straps like soldiers. In fact, the first time that Slocum saw them come in the cantina, he thought they were *federales*.

When the pack train guards weren't in town, he flirted with Donna. She loved to dance and show herself off, clacking castanets and stomping her heels around a hat on the tile floor while Ramon played the trumpet.

Slocum sat back and watched her firm cleavage shake in the low-cut dress, and enjoyed watching her slim hips connected to high heels stomp at the floor to the beat of the music. She was on wings when she danced. That was why she charged more than the other girls. Why she had the best dresses of all the *putas* in this bar. She was the flashy-eyed one who drew men like flowers drew bees and always wanted to be "raped."

She brushed her hair the next morning seated on the bed. Even when she did such a task, it was done as hard as she danced. She wanted no tangles, no restraint to the bristles, or she swore pulling through them. He knew, lying naked on his belly in the still-warm bed beside her, that it must hurt to pull that hard—it was her way.

"Where will you go today?" she asked as if it perturbed her.

"To a rancheria in the mountains. To look at some horses."

She gave him a haughty glance. "Do you have money to buy fancy horses?"

"No. I'm going to look at them for another man. He has money."

"Will he pay you well?" She tied her long black hair back with a ribbon.

He nodded and yawned.

"You could stay here today. Obregon's pack train people won't be back here until Thursday. Then you could go to the fucking mountains."

"Mountains do that?"

"No, but you seem to like to."

He scratched his scalp. "You saying we could stay in bed all day if I put off going to look at those horses?"

"Yes. Yes." She turned around and began attacking him with the hairbrush. The blue silk shift fell open, and he could see her tight tits shaking as he restrained her arms from striking him and she struggled to hit him some more.

Damn, he had a hellcat. He wrestled her down on her back in the bed. She rolled and tossed to escape being underneath him. Her dark eyes shot darts of anger at him, and Spanish words came from her mouth as she called him a seducer of his own mother. With her white teeth gritted, she tried to knee him in the balls, but he avoided the attempt, using his weight to press her down.

Then he forced her slender legs apart with his knee and she arched her back to escape him. But she was not quick enough for him now, and he had her legs parted and he was hunching his half-hard dick at her with a fury. He struck pay dirt and she screamed "No!" at his entry.

Then she threw the brush away and clutched him like a drowning person in a swift river. He sought the depth of her, plunging in and out wildly with his hardening shaft. He was lying on top of her hard breasts, clutching her buttocks in each hand as he screwed her for all he was worth.

The world swirled around him, his breath rasped in his throat. She bit him on the chest not once, but several times. Hard enough to draw blood. He grew so fierce with her, she began to moan and toss her head, begging him to come. Then, at last, he felt the rising fountain and pressed as hard as he could into her.

She raised her butt off the bed, clutched him, and screamed, "Yes!" Then she slid into a faint.

He didn't go look at horses that day or the next. Thursday, he passed the stiff-looking guards and their long file of mules as he rode up the mountain on his quest to buy mares for Don Montoya. Under their strict orders, none of the guards so much as recognized him. They were on the alert for bandits—anything that might endanger the train. When they passed him in their long trot headed for Portis, he rode on up to Sorrell's Rancheria.

Sorrell's wife Magdalena had lunch ready, and opened the door when he came on the porch. An attractive woman in her early forties, she wore a sweeping dress and caught his arm. "Lunch is ready for you. But you have come two days late. My husband has gone to Mexico City, so you have missed him."

"Forgive me. I was detained."

She stopped in the doorway to the dining room and looked him over. "Not in jail, I hope."

"No."

"Well, it is much more interesting to have you here without Phillip anyway."

He kissed her. They lingered in the doorway for a long

while tasting each other, before she pulled him over to the table of food.

"So much food," he said, looking over the spread.

"You better eat well, I have big plans for you." She pressed her breasts against his arm and smiled like a fox.

"Señora! Señor! There is a boy here says he must see the señor."

"What for?' She looked displeased at the interruption.

"I better go see," he said. "I'll be right back." What could be wrong in Mexico to take him away from an afternoon with her?

Taking leave of his hostess, he followed the out-of-breath hefty housekeeper through the tile hallways to the courtyard, and there a familiar boy named Pancho sat upon a lathered horse. The anxiousness in his dark eyes told Slocum something was bad wrong.

"Oh, Señor, Armando sends for you. Banditos robbed the pack train today in Portis and they have killed most of the guards."

"*Gracias,* I'll get my horse and ride for there at once. I must tell the lady I am leaving." And he dreaded that.

"Ah, what was it?" she asked, coming down the hallway to meet him.

"I have to go. Bandits robbed the ore pack train and they need me."

"What for? Obregon has tons more ore in his rich mine." The look of impatience swept her face as she waited for his reply.

"My friend Armando has asked for my help. I will go help him."

"But what about me? I need help too."

He drew a deep breath and made certain they were alone. Satisfied no one was in the hall, he swept her in his arms and kissed her—hard. When their mouths parted, she sighed and put her forehead on his chest in surrender. "All right, if you must go. Don't forget to come back."

"No, ma'am. I won't."

He pushed Sarge hard for Portis. At dark, he reached it, had a stable boy walk Roan dry, and found a bandaged-up guard in uniform seated at a table by himself in the cantina. He introduced himself as Salarus and shook his head in defeat when Slocum joined him.

"Where is your boss?"

"Dead like the rest."

"Who was it did this?"

Armando, in a fresh white apron, joined them. "I have sent word to Obregon. But he will be another day getting my message. These men have been good customers of mine. I will miss them all. They killed seven of them, and I thought maybe since the banditos are gringos you could run them down."

"Who did this?"

"A Colonel Williams and his men."

"Williams?" Slocum shook his head in disbelief. What was he going to do with gold ore anyway?

"*Sí.*"

"What did he want gold ore for?"

Armando looked at Salarus and the man nodded. "Why—" Armando lowered his voice. "We can't tell everyone. It was not all gold ore. That ore you can take across the border has no tax. This had gold bars as well under the ore. You savvy?"

Slocum nodded as he looked across the cantina at the dust dancing in the shaft of light. That was why Willams wanted it. "Which way did they ride?"

Armando pointed north and then looked hard at Slocum. "See why we could not tell the authorities?"

Slocum nodded, considering all of the things he needed to do. They had a two-day start on him.

"I know Obregon will pay you well." Armando said. "He is a very rich man."

"I can ride with you," Salarus said.

Slocum looked at the bandaged man and shook his head. "I'm not a doctor. You better stay here."

"But they are a tough bunch—they took us by surprise."

"That's what I plan to try."

"But—I could get you some pistoleros from around here."

"I'd not dare trust them. Get me two of those good horses that the guards rode and saddle both of them. I want four sticks of blasting powder, caps, and cord too. I'll leave Sarge here. You look out for him."

"*Sí*, but these men—"

"I know them. They aren't that tough."

"If anything happens to you . . ." Armando wadded the apron in his hands.

"Get me some food too," Slocum added.

"No problem." Armando ran off.

"Now tell me all about the robbery," he said to Salarus.

"We were in camp when they struck. . . ."

The sunset's last bloody rays knifed across the desert. The shadows grew longer by the minute and small mountains became dark-sided as the daylight shrunk. Slocum rode one of the fine powerful horses in a hard lope and led the other at his right side. Every hour he switched mounts without dismounting, simply slipped off one and onto the other while they ran. If his plan worked, he should overtake the pack train by sunup.

His biggest concern was running into them in the middle of the night. It was a chance he had to take—they would hurry like a house afire to get over the border to escape any Mexican law. Then, in Texas, they'd settle down and laugh at their good fortune—maybe even celebrate. That was where he hoped to overtake them—celebrating their success.

He crossed the shallow Rio Grande and saw the flickering lights of Red Star, Texas. The small village was home to many smugglers, and he expected to find Willams among them. When his horses stopped and shook hard on the sandy bank of American soil, he turned an ear and heard a jackass bray. Not a burro, but a mule's large throaty rasping bray.

They were there. He headed for the livery corral, and could see in the shadowy light the loaded mules in the pen.

So as not to draw attention, he rode on past and went behind some jacales to dismount. When his horses were hitched securely, he made his way back to spy on the pack animals.

Who was guarding them? No one? No one. Getting those mules to run would be impossible, especially by himself. So he didn't stand a chance of stealing them and outrunning the crew, even with their spent horses. He needed to settle this with the big man, Williams—but how and where?

Williams's run-hard and put-away-wet crew must be tired. They might be asleep or drunk. This could be his chance to slip in and reduce their numbers. His shoulder against the adobe corner of the jacal, he watched a woman coming from the back door of the cantina. She wrapped herself in a blanket against the night chill and hurried toward where Slocum stood in the darkness.

He caught her and clamped a hand over her mouth, dragging her back in the darkness. "Easy, lady, I won't hurt you," he said in her ear. "I need information. Is the colonel in there?"

She nodded and he eased his hand off her lips. "Sorry, but they killed some men in Mexico. How many are in there?"

She held up her fingers on one hand at him.

"Fine. Is the colonel drunk?" he whispered in her ear.

"*Sí.*"

"How about the others?"

"They are all drunk."

In his saddlebags were four armed sticks of blasting powder. If he— "Who else is in there?"

"Two *putas* and the man owns the bar, Cortez."

"Can you get those two out?"

"I don't know." She trembled.

"Tell them to come quick, someone is having a baby."

"But what if they won't come?"

"I don't want them caught in the cross fire."

She nodded woodenly. "How long do I have?"

"A few minutes. Can you hurry?"

She agreed, and hurried back toward the cantina. He had

to hope she didn't tip the bandits off. When she disappeared inside, he went to the back wall and began to drill a hole with his skinning knife in the adobe to set the stick. Number one was soon packed in about head-high on him; the second one was easily bored next and set about six feet away.

Too his relief, the three women soon came out and rushed off in the dark. Chattering away in Spanish about birthing problems, they headed away from the cantina. He lit both fuses and then hurried around in front. From across the street, he could see the lighted interior.

He ducked when the explosion went off and belched a great blast of dirt out the open doorway. Then, in the starlight, the "deaf" outlaws spilled into the street, cursing and quizzing each other who'd farted that bad.

"Shuck your guns. Hands in the air or you all die. There are five rifles pointed at you."

"Okay. Okay," came their replies. Guns dropped in the dirt and men emerged from the relative darkness with their hands raised high. They moved into the center of the street peering around for him and *his army*.

"How did you find us?"

"I followed the horse biscuits. Where's the colonel?"

"Right here, you sumbitch!" The red flare from his pistol muzzle came from the doorway.

Slocum's .44 answered him twice. There is a sound of impact when a bullet solidly strikes a body like a thump on a watermelon—both Slocum's shots sounded that way. Williams's next round went into the dirt as he crumpled to his knees and went facedown.

"You all better run west. My men'll start shooting at the count of five. One . . . Two . . ." They fled and he was alone.

"Señor, gracias," a woman said in a soft voice from the shadows.

He tipped his hat and went for his horses. It would be a long drive back without help. He'd find out how generous Obregon really was. And there was Donna, my, my.

He shook his sleep-deprived head and blinked his dry

gritty eyes. Maybe he could slip up and be there in Abilene
in the spring. Better get them mules rolling.

Early June in Kansas, and the wind whipped the prairie
flowers in bloom. The fresh-cut pine boards on Joe McCoy's
new cattle pens smelled like turpentine. Slocum was drinking good whiskey from the neck of a bottle and passing it
around. One-eyed Paco, grinning like a tomcat that had just
topped a female in heat, took his turn at swigging it down.
And working on a tablet with a pencil, dressed in his snow-
white shirt, black tie, and small black hat on the back of his
head, Hertz was figuring numbers.

"It has been a long damn ways up here from Texas, *mi
amigo*."

"Ought to make you lots of money."

Hertz looked up at them as if amazed. "It really did."

"Sounds like the Estrella Cattle Company is in business."

"Yes, thanks to you. What do you need?" Paco asked
Slocum. "What can I do for you?"

"A couple of fresh plain horses, and fifty bucks. I ran
mine in the ground to get up here in time."

"Amigo, I am a little short—" Paco teased, and then
broke out laughing. He clapped Slocum on the shoulder,
which raised a cloud of dust. "I'm sure glad you came by for
this day. We got Mary on her farm in Texas too."

Slocum nodded. He knew all about her, he'd been by to
check on her. "Matt ain't in this world anymore either."

"Good. The colonel?"

"He killed him. Told me so." That was enough. There was
something happening out there in the West, new places he
needed to see. He'd be heading that way when the sun came
up, unless some Abilene doxie forced him at gunpoint to
stay in her bed.

Watch for

SLOCUM IN SHOT CREEK

344th novel in the exciting SLOCUM series
from Jove

Coming in October!

Jove Westerns put the "wild"
back into the Wild West.

LONGARM
by Tabor Evans

THE GUNSMITH
by
J.R. Roberts

SLOCUM by
JAKE LOGAN

Don't miss these exciting, all-action series!

penguin.com

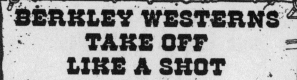